"That's the first sound Cody has made with me," Elise said with a smile.

"But you said he can communicate." Jack remembered her mentioning it on the first day.

"He could before the accident."

"And now he doesn't." Jack's empathy toward the boy intensified. Yes, Jack had lost his family, too, but he'd only withdrawn from society. Cody had withdrawn from everything.

"Now he doesn't," she repeated softly.

"Without speaking, I'm guessing the chances for an autistic boy to be adopted are slim to nil," Jack deduced.

Elise didn't answer, but her silence said everything. The boy needed to communicate in order to stand a chance at a family wanting to adopt him.

Pondering Cody's situation and what he could do to help, Jack carefully maintained his distance from the woman in his kitchen.

He didn't want to stand too close, didn't want to be too close. But he also needed her to understand that he didn't want to stop seeing Cody.

Today was the first day Jack had felt alive in a very long time.

Renee Andrews spends a lot of time in the gym. No, she isn't working out. Her husband, a former All-American gymnast, co-owns ACE Cheer Company. Renee is a kidney donor and actively supports organ donation. When she isn't writing, she enjoys traveling with her husband and bragging about their sons, daughter-in-law and grandsons. For more info on her books or on living donors, visit her website at reneeandrews.com.

Books by Renee Andrews

Love Inspired

Willow's Haven

Family Wanted
Second Chance Father

Her Valentine Family
Healing Autumn's Heart
Picture Perfect Family
Love Reunited
Heart of a Rancher
Bride Wanted
Yuletide Twins
Mommy Wanted
Small-Town Billionaire
Daddy Wanted

Visit the Author Profile page at Harlequin.com for more titles.

Second Chance Father

Renee Andrews

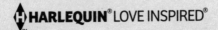

HARLEQUIN® LOVE INSPIRED®

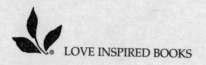

LOVE INSPIRED BOOKS

Recycling programs for this product may not exist in your area.

ISBN-13: 978-0-373-89906-7

Second Chance Father

Printed in U.S.A.

The Lord is a refuge for the oppressed,
a stronghold in times of trouble. Those who know
Your name trust in You, for You, Lord,
have never forsaken those who seek You.
—*Psalms* 9:9–10

The past year has blessed our family
with three precious new grandbabies.
This book is dedicated to them:
Brooks McCallum, Naomi Zeringue
and Konrad Zeringue. Pops and KK love you,
big as the sky, to the moon and back!

Acknowledgments

Tremendous thanks to my editor, Shana Asaro,
for her understanding and guidance in helping
me best portray the story and characters
that are so near and dear to my heart.

Kelly Mooney, thank you so much for insight into
your world. When I realized I'd be meeting an
honest-to-goodness LA producer three years ago,
I didn't know God was providing a new friend.
You're amazing, and I truly hope
you'll come see us in Alabama again!

Emily Hausmann Hill, I remember the first time
I met you, when you brought three precious
children to our home for fostering. You truly care
about each and every child you've helped place
over the years, and our family was blessed to
have you as our social worker. Thank you
for your guidance in Elise's character.

As always, any and all errors
are completely mine.

Chapter One

A dark-haired boy stood at the edge of Jack Simon's property.

Yesterday, when Jack first saw the child near the woods, he'd believed his grief had finally taken its toll on his mind. He'd bought this cabin specifically for the location, far enough away from civilization that he'd never be reminded of everything he'd lost—not the wife who loved him with the kind of adoration he attempted to portray on the silver screen, or the twin girls who made his heart soar with their uninhibited giggles, or the son...

The boy looked as real as the woman Jack had fabricated last week during his morning run. He'd never encountered anyone in that time, when daylight barely touched the forest and the trail was as desolate as his soul, but that day, he'd envisioned a striking woman, her arms wrapped around her stomach as she curled into herself, rocking through the pain of her sobs.

Dark chestnut hair veiled her face until she must have sensed she'd been spotted and peered through the woods toward Jack. Even with tears streaming down her cheeks, she'd been one of the most beautiful women he'd ever seen. Olive skin. Doe eyes. A full mouth curved down with sadness.

Angry he'd allowed himself to betray Laney's memory with the alluring vision, Jack had increased his speed, running with such abandon that he left the path and lost himself in the dense woods, where the canopy of trees blocked out every ounce of light.

He had no idea how long he ran that morning, not that it mattered. It wasn't like he had anywhere to be at any certain time.

Another reason he'd moved here.

The boy tapped his fingers together at his chest. If Jack *were* imagining a child, would he look so detailed, with his head cocked to the side as though he were confused to find Jack in the middle of the woods, instead of the other way around? And if Jack *had* dreamed up a kid that looked ten years old, the same age as Jack Jr. had been, wouldn't the boy be sandy-haired, like his son? Or have that easy smile and those deep dimples that always graced JJ's face? This boy's mouth stretched flat, not quite in a frown, but closer to a grimace than a smile.

Then again, the woman he concocted hadn't looked like Laney, either. His beloved wife, with her white-blond curls and fair skin making her appear even more innocent on their wedding day. The woman in the woods contrasted with Laney in every way, from her tan skin to her dark hair to the torment etched on her face.

The boy shook his head, as though he'd decided he was in the wrong place, or that Jack wasn't who he'd planned to see this deep in the woods.

It'd been a long time, at least three or four days, since Jack had been required to mutter a word, but sensing the boy was about to flee, he cleared his throat and called out, "Hey! Do you live around here?" An odd question, since Jack hadn't seen any other homes nearby. But he assumed there could be more places like this tucked within the thick forests that blanketed North Alabama's Lookout Mountains.

Maybe the boy camped with his family near

Jasper Falls. Jack supposed schools could be out for fall break, since it was the third week of October. But Jasper Falls was at least four miles away. Chances were the kid had wandered farther than he realized. JJ had done that once, when Jack had been shooting *The Journey* on location near Prague. Laney had been frantic with worry when they couldn't find their son. So had Jack.

And the joy they'd experienced when JJ had been found spurred the idea for *Finding Home,* a film that would be released in two months, on Christmas Day. The last picture Jack would ever direct.

And a premiere he'd never see.

He swallowed thickly, wiped a sleeve against his brow and squinted toward the kid again. "Are you…lost or something?" He could ask himself the same question. Lost. Out of his mind. Out of his element. It'd been two years since that plane went down. Everyone had claimed he'd be normal after one.

Of course, Jack had never been accused of being normal.

But in spite of the concerns from his friends, his parents and every studio in LA, he'd found the most remote place to live. Away from the pain. Away from every reminder of the past.

And then…this boy.

Jack stopped sanding the slab of wood destined to be the side of his dresser and removed the wide plank from the table saw. He needed to determine what to do about the boy. Pulling his cell phone from his pocket, he prepared to let the authorities know about the child wandering the woods. Then he glanced toward the trees and, like yesterday, the kid disappeared as quickly as he'd come.

A sudden urge to pray for the boy's safety—and his own sanity—coaxed Jack's brain, but he swallowed past the impulse that had once been second nature. God wasn't listening, and Jack still had serious doubts about whether the child even existed. No need to call the police to announce he'd lost his mind. Besides, escaping civilization didn't include broadcasting his residence in the woods. So far, he'd managed to stay clear of the townsfolk in Claremont, the tiny community fifteen miles away. Keeping his distance would be a lot easier if he didn't summon the cops to his house.

He grabbed his thermos from the porch, took a long drink of ice water and let the liquid cool his throat and settle his spirit. "He must have been a figment of my imagination." Saying the words aloud helped to reassure himself, as did selecting the next piece of wood. Surely staying busy would keep the illusions at bay.

The thick plank of mahogany held its weight well, and Jack liked knowing that he would create a piece that would last for generations. Not that he'd have any subsequent generations to continue the Simon name.

"Hello?" The lyrical voice, undeniably female, provided a stark contrast to Jack's present frustration. He relaxed his grip on the mahogany and turned toward the spot where the kid had been.

The woman from the woods—the exquisite lady from his dreams—gingerly stepped over a cluster of tree roots as she edged into the clearing.

What would he imagine next, twin girls with pale blond pigtails and eyes that sparkled when they laughed? Jack closed his eyes, inhaled deeply and embraced the reminder of reality. The scents of fresh sawdust, crisp pine and damp earth. Then, exhaling slowly, he listened to the haunting sounds of the slight wind pushing through the trees.

Several long moments passed.

He finally opened his eyes, expecting the hallucination to be gone.

Still there.

In case this wasn't a delusion, Jack cleared his throat and repeated, "Hello." His voice came out as coarse and grainy as he felt, and the woman's widened eyes and hand to her heart showed her shock at his near-growl.

No doubt about it, this wasn't a dream. She was as real as the heavy slab of wood in his hands.

He made another attempt. "Sorry. I'm… not…used to visitors."

Her head moved in a subtle nod, but she stopped progressing toward him, which Jack understood. He hadn't showered yet today and it had been weeks since he'd shaved. His hand drifted to his face, fingers scrubbing across a thick, wiry mass of beard.

When was the last time he'd actually looked in the mirror?

The golden afternoon sunlight sliced through the trees and shimmered against her pretty brown hair as she took a step forward. She wore a button-up sheer floral blouse over a peach T-shirt, extremely feminine, but also outdoorsy when paired with her dark blue jeans and hiking boots. Shoving her hands in her pockets, she peered toward his log cabin, then scanned the area to his right, and then his left, regarding him as more of an obstruction than an asset to her obvious search.

Jack suspected he knew what—or rather, who—she wanted to see.

Determined to make his voice less gruff, he cleared his throat. "You looking for a young boy?"

One arched brow shot up, eyes widening even more, and her jaw tensed. "Have you seen him? Is he okay?"

He thought about his old flannel shirt, the sleeves pushed up to the elbows and covered with sawdust. The equally worn jeans that were his favorite, because his kids had given them to him on the last Father's Day he celebrated. And the work boots he'd bought when he decided to live the rest of his days in solitude, disappearing in what he'd thought to be uninhabited terrain, in North Alabama, of all places.

Maybe he *was* crazy. And maybe, considering his unkempt state of dress, he looked like an ax murderer.

At least he wasn't holding a chain saw.

"I didn't hurt him," he said, which, judging from her reaction, may not have been the smartest thing to say.

* * *

Elise Ramsey didn't know what she expected to find when she'd gone searching for Cody in the woods, beyond finding the boy, that is. But she certainly hadn't expected to happen upon this big, burly guy in the middle of the forest. "You didn't hurt him?"

What did *that* mean? And where was Cody now? She continued scanning the area around the log cabin but saw no sign of her patient.

"No, I didn't." He placed a huge plank of wood across two sawhorses and swiped a sleeve across his forehead. "He was here, and I tried to talk to him, but he didn't respond."

"He wouldn't have. He can't." She closed her eyes and said a prayer for the boy. He'd disappeared yesterday at the same time, during the late-afternoon devotional, when the kids of Willow's Haven all gathered at the fire pit to be reminded of God's place in their lives and that they were all loved and wanted. Something many of them couldn't say about their lives before.

"He *can't*?" His head tilted, forehead wrinkled in confusion. "Can't speak?"

Elise silently scolded herself for letting her rattled disposition interfere with her natural filter regarding her patient. But she hadn't told this bearded stranger anything that she couldn't share. Anyone who encountered Cody learned quickly enough that he'd stopped speaking. "He can," she corrected, "but he doesn't. Not anymore. Or at least not yet." Hopefully she'd make progress with the child she'd already grown to care so much about, and he *would* find his voice again.

"He stopped talking?" The man pushed his sleeves up and then crossed his arms in a move that brought her attention to muscled forearms. Bulging biceps. And the extent of just how much larger he was than Cody. Or Elise. "What happened to him?" he asked.

Did he know? Was Cody still here?

A frisson of fear shimmied down her spine, but she held her ground. Cody was her responsibility, and she needed to verify that he was okay. This guy said he didn't hurt Cody, but he certainly looked like he could hurt someone. Granted, she'd never spent any time in the woods before her current placement at Willow's Haven, but even if she had, she wouldn't have expected to run upon a man who looked like he'd been dropped out of the Wild West. Minus the horses. And the guns.

She hoped.

God, please, keep Cody safe.

"Where is he?" Elise hated that her voice trembled on the last word and said another quick prayer for courage.

The man unfolded his arms, moved a palm to his forehead and then pinched the bridge of his nose as though warding off a migraine. The action looked more like something she'd expect from someone sitting behind a desk than a rough-hewn fellow in the woods. Finally, he spoke, but his voice didn't spark the fear it had before. "I don't know where he is. I tried to talk to him and he ran off."

"Where was he? Where did you see him, exactly?" She needed a clue on where to find Cody. Had he returned to Willow's Haven, like before, or had he wandered deeper into the forest?

He pointed toward the woods. "There, same place he showed up yesterday. Disappeared right before you got here."

That got her attention. "He came here yesterday?" She pulled her hands from her pockets and planted them on her hips. "You didn't try to find out why an eleven-year-old was wandering the woods? Didn't think you should call the police?" If he had, she would have known where Cody had been yesterday, or where he might go again. Like he'd done today. "You didn't think someone would want to know that he was here? In the middle of nowhere?"

He took a deep breath, and her attention moved to the hard outline of his chest, easily visible in spite of his loose flannel shirt. The guy was built, but she didn't notice in an oh-how-rugged kind of way. Rather, she noticed in a he's-strong-and-could-hurt-someone kind of way.

The broad shoulders lifted and then fell. "I wasn't sure he was real." His words seemed to surprise himself as much as Elise, and she merely stood there, mouth agape, and wondered how to respond.

He wasn't sure Cody was *real*?

"Unbelievable." Clearly, trying to converse with this mountain of a man wasn't helping her find her young patient, so she turned and started down the trail. He'd found his way back yesterday; maybe he'd done the same today. And if Mountain Man planned to hurt her, he could just start coming. He was big, but she was fast, and she'd give him a good run for his money through the woods. Besides, she didn't have time to waste chatting. She had to find Cody before dark.

"Wait."

The urgency in his deep voice caused her to stop and look over her shoulder at the man making his way across the area cleared for the cabin. Elise had been surprised to find the opening in the thickest section of trees earlier, but she wasn't surprised that Cody had found it. The boy's intelligence was astounding.

"Yeah?" She watched him as he neared. He wasn't as massive as she'd originally thought. Muscled, yes. Bulky, no. He appeared ultra-healthy, though, like the CrossFit junkies that lived in her apartment complex in Birmingham. And in spite of the thick beard, his skin was smooth, with a tanned complexion that showcased eyes that were the most intriguing color she'd ever seen. Sea-foam green.

She tried to picture him without the beard.

"No need to be scared of me." He focused on her as he spoke, and she watched his eyes soften, as though he somehow knew how much she'd been through and how very much she wanted to help the child who'd wandered away again. He took a deep breath, let it out and added, "I know I look rough, but…"

"I'm not…scared of you." The words were true. A guy ends up being attractive and having sensitive eyes, and she gives him the green light to walk up and start talking. Her brothers would have a serious problem with her measuring stick for safe guys she encountered in the jungle. Woods. Whatever. But that'd always been Elise's problem, the desire to help those who were socially off centered. It'd been the reason for her choice of profession, the fact that her father didn't fit in the world. And then it'd been the reason for her marriage.

She blinked, the reminder serving its purpose. The last thing she needed was another guy who had social issues. And this man, who willingly set up house in the middle of nowhere, definitely fell into that category.

He cleared his throat, nodded his head toward her as though making a decision. "Don't worry. I'll help you find your son."

For a moment, she thought he'd gone crazy. But then she remembered he had no way of knowing the truth and that she needed to get back on track and find Cody instead of talking to an unsavory mountain man. "He isn't my son. He's my patient."

Her phone buzzed before he could respond, and she slid the cell out of her jeans to glance at the text message from Savvy Evans.

Cody just got back. Seems fine.

Relief washed through her. "He's back," she said. "At Willow's Haven. Cody is okay."

"Willow's Haven?"

How could he live this close to the place and not know of its existence? "The children's home, about a half mile west of here."

"He's your patient?" Confusion etched through his words.

"I'm a licensed social worker specializing in autism spectrum disorders, and I'm currently working at Willow's Haven. I'm here specifically for Cody." Saying it stabbed her heart, because this was the first case where she had made absolutely no progress after two weeks of intense therapy.

But Elise knew Cody was at the right place. Willow's Haven would give him more personalized attention than any of the state-funded homes. "I'm beginning to wonder if I'm the right person for the job." She hadn't divulged that to Brodie, Savvy or even her colleagues at the Birmingham Clinic for Autism. Maybe the fact that she was in the middle of nowhere, and that she'd probably never see this guy again, gave her freedom to give voice to her fear.

"What's wrong with him?" His voice had

taken on a different tone than before, still as deep, but compassionate too.

"I can't tell you anything patient-specific, but since he is at the children's home, it's common knowledge that he lost his family."

"How?" The word came out thick and raspy. "How did he lose his family?"

She needed to get back to Willow's Haven, but the concern in his masculine tone caused her to answer. "A car crash. Cody was the sole survivor."

A shadow passed over his face, a look of sadness, or longing. Merely a flicker of emotion, but Elise saw it.

He turned his attention to the tree branches shifting overhead, and the thick cords of his neck pulsed as he swallowed. "He lost his family."

Her background gave her a keen sense at reading people. This man had been hard to interpret at a distance, but now that he stood so close, she could tell from the tiny twitch beneath his eye that he worked hard to keep his emotions in check.

She suddenly wanted to know more about this mysterious stranger who lived in the woods. Glancing at his left hand, she saw no ring. And then she mentally stopped that train of thought. She lived in Birmingham and had a great practice there. This was a special case that would have her staying at Willow's Haven for a time, and then she'd leave. Moving away from Cody. And away from the big, sensitive mountain man undeniably similar to the last guy who'd captured her heart. Then shattered it.

"I'm Jack."

She'd been so absorbed in the painful memory that she had missed part of his conversation. But now that he'd offered his first name, she waited to see if he'd give her the last one too.

He didn't.

Elise sighed. She needed to get back to the issue at hand, taking care of Cody, and not the fact that the last guy she'd given her heart to made her a widow at twenty-eight. "Well, Jack, if Cody comes this way again, can you make sure he gets back to Willow's Haven?" She pointed to the right fork of the trail ahead of her. "Down that way." It wasn't a clear path, but it was manageable, obviously, since Cody found his way through the woods and to Jack's cabin.

"There wasn't an orphanage there when I bought my place."

Elise was used to the misconception about the home. "Willow's Haven isn't an orphanage, even though some of the children have been orphaned. A children's home differs in that it provides a safe sanctuary for children who are without a family, for any reason."

And then she focused on what else he'd said. "Willow's Haven has been open for a year now. When did you buy your place?"

"Nearly two years ago." Another look passed over his face, and she read it clearly. Sadness. More specifically, grief.

What—or who—had this man lost?

"You've been living here for two years?" Why would anyone choose to live like this? "By yourself?" she added and then wished she'd kept that query silenced.

"No, I bought it two years ago, but I only recently moved in. I had to—" he paused "—take care of a few things first."

And *that* made her wonder what things had taken two years to take care of. And what kind of job allowed him to live out here in the middle of nowhere, where only one cellular company managed to provide service, and even that was spotty at best. "But you're planning to live here, long-term?"

He nodded and offered no additional information. "Do you want me to call you if I see the lad again?"

Normally she'd have thought of that from the get-go, but being this close to the guy rattled her senses. "That'd be great." She didn't have a card on her, hadn't anticipated running into anyone when she headed into the woods after Cody. But she needn't have worried about having a card.

He slid long fingers into his jeans pocket to withdraw his cell, then asked, "What's your number?"

Alarms blared through her head, all initiated from years of warnings from her three older brothers, but even so, she recited her number and watched him key it into his phone. Probably the easiest set of digits the man had ever received.

She felt weird surrendering her contact information like that. But she didn't give out her number to just any guy who asked. Besides, it wasn't like he'd suggested they go out to dinner together. Or that he ever would.

"I'll call you if I see him…" He let the word hang and then lifted the phone to show the empty contact field on the display. "But I still need your name."

"Elise," she said. "Elise Ramsey."

He entered it into the appropriate box. "Got it."

She took a step back and, bizarrely, found herself not quite ready to leave. But her patient was at Willow's Haven, which meant she should get there too. "I've got to go see to Cody." She walked away from the guy who'd taken her by complete surprise, both with his appearance in the forest and with the effect he had on her senses.

"I want to help him too."

Elise tripped over a tree root, stumbled, but caught herself before falling completely, and then she pivoted to see the guy whose words had rocked her to the core.

He stood grounded to the spot, raising his brow as though waiting for her to tell him how he could help.

"That's real nice of you." She struggled to figure this man out. First he scared her to death, then he admitted that her patient had been to see him—twice. And now he asked to help said patient. "But I'm not sure what you could do."

Oak leaves crunched beneath his feet as he took the few steps needed to lessen the gap between them. He stopped just shy of her three feet of personal space, which was good. The sky had darkened as late afternoon turned to early evening, and she still didn't know a whole lot about the man. Except that he was big and rugged. Socially challenged. And even more attractive up close.

"He must be interested in my cabin, or in the furniture I'm building, or something. Maybe I can use that to break down his barrier and get him to talk."

Elise homed in on the part he'd said that would potentially interest Cody. "I'd almost forgotten. His father was a carpenter. Is that your occupation too?"

"No. I worked in the film industry." The slight shake of his head at the end of the sentence told Elise he wished he hadn't told her that much. "You think he came around because he saw me building furniture?"

She decided to leave the film industry comment alone. She wasn't here to get information about Jack; she needed to stay focused on her patient. "From what I've read about Cody's history, his interests never aligned with his father's occupation." She would've left it at that, but he seemed to drink in every tidbit about the boy, so she explained, "Cody is an autistic savant."

His head tilted. "Like Dustin Hoffman in *Rain Man*?"

Elise sighed. As much as that movie didn't portray the vast scope of the savant syndrome, it did do much in alerting the general public to the specialized care needed by those individuals diagnosed with the disorder. "Cody is similar to that," she said, "but his area of expertise is rather unique. Dustin Hoffman's character specialized in math. Cody specializes in cars."

"Cars?"

"Specifically the muscle cars of the sixties."

Awareness coated his features, and the right corner of his mouth crooked up at the edge. "He's had on a classic car shirt both times I've seen him."

"And he'll have another one on if you see him again. That's all he'll wear." She heard a branch crack behind her and jerked around so fast that she lost her balance.

A large palm caught her left bicep and steadied her before she fell.

"You okay?" His face hovered near to hers. So close that she could see genuine concern in those uniquely colored green eyes.

Her personal space was officially invaded, big-time, resulting in her heart traipsing into a nice gallop. "I'm…fine." She eased away from the warmth of his hand. "I should get back to Willow's Haven, and to Cody."

"I meant what I said, about helping him," Jack stated firmly. "If his dad was a carpenter, then he can help me out with the furniture I'm building. Maybe that'll let him cope with the loss somehow."

Anything that would get Cody to ease out of his shell would be progress, but Elise doubted carpentry would do the trick, based on his prior caseworker's files. "I'm not sure…"

"If that doesn't work, I have another idea." He gave her a moment to respond. When she didn't, he added, "You should let me try. I know what he's going through."

Her phone buzzed in her pocket, and she withdrew it to see another text from Savvy.

Pretty sure Cody is looking for you.

She wanted to ask Jack what he meant. How did he know what Cody was going through? He'd assumed Willow's Haven was an orphanage. Had he been orphaned too? Was *that* why he'd decided to remove himself from society, remain holed up in middle-of-nowhere, Alabama?

"Bring him back tomorrow. Let me help." His words were almost delivered as a command, and Elise wondered what kind of position of authority this guy held in the past that he believed people would do his bidding simply because he stated it.

Even so, she wanted to help Cody. Needed to. And the boy did seem drawn to this guy. Then again, she'd be lying if she said she wasn't drawn to him too. There was something about him…

She cleared her head, thought about what was best for her patient. "It'd be better if Cody came back on his own, instead of me trying to force him to do anything."

"Okay. But I think he will."

Elise nodded. Cody had been here twice in two days. There was no reason to think he wouldn't make an effort to return again tomorrow. "I do too."

He gave her a slight smile, as though pleased she gave the right answer, and, again, she wondered what kind of power this man had held—or still held—in his world. Showing her his phone, he added, "I'll call you when he does." Then he indicated the path behind Elise. "You should probably go before the rain."

"What rain?" she asked, as a loud boom of thunder in the distance made her jump, and then a heavy drop of water plopped on her nose.

"I've always sensed when storms are coming." His voice rumbled almost as fiercely as the sounds echoing from the dark clouds overhead.

"Call me if you see him again." More drops plopped on her head, and she became aware of the musty odor and heaviness permeating the air. Then she turned and darted down the trail but chanced one more look over her shoulder to see Jack, standing in the rain, watching her disappear into the woods as if he wanted to make sure she made it back safely.

Why did she have the impulse to turn around, run the opposite direction...and make sure he found his way home too?

Chapter Two

Jack sat on the front steps of his cabin and watched the how-to video on his laptop. Before yesterday, he'd have sat inside to view the next steps involved in building a seven-drawer dresser, but now that he knew the boy he'd encountered actually existed, he didn't want to miss his reappearance. In fact, he had a difficult time paying attention to the video, because he couldn't keep his gaze from wandering to that spot in the woods where Cody had appeared.

And then Elise.

Throughout the night and most of today, he'd found himself thinking as much about the woman as the boy. Or more. He'd been impressed with her willingness to approach him, a stranger, in order to find and protect her son.

No, not her son, her patient. *That* had surprised him, the way she'd shown so much motherly instinct toward a child for which she shared no blood bond. A beautiful thing, really. In another place and time, he would've taken that exquisite situation, the layers of emotions, peeled them away from the surface and studied them, then analyzed the best way to portray a woman who cared so deeply on the big screen.

Gritting his teeth at the way his mind always went *there*, he stopped thinking about the large screens of the past and instead turned his attention to the small screen in front of him, the one showing a master woodworker describing how to build the drawers. But Jack hadn't finished the frame, and he'd glazed over during the applicable part, his thoughts on the grieving boy and intriguing woman instead of his current task.

He restarted the last section of the video and watched it again. The simple action of repeating the segment brought back a memory of JJ, standing outside Hollywood's ArcLight Cinemas at the prescreening of *The Journey*.

Dad, what happens when someone has to leave to go to the bathroom or something?

How do they know what they missed without talking during the show?

Jack had laughed that the boy, only six or seven at the time, already knew the rules of silence during those screenings. Then he'd explained that most often the audience could determine what they'd missed by the foreshadowing layered throughout the earlier frames, or by the dialogue or actions in the scenes that followed. Or they could simply buy another ticket and see the movie again. That last portion of Jack's answer had been overheard by a reporter and included in reviews about the film. JJ had been thrilled to have had a part in the written reviews.

And Jack had looked forward to the day when he'd see his son following in his footsteps.

Ready to begin working and get his mind off the past, he shut the computer. He'd watched the portion on building the frame several times already and knew he wouldn't make it much further than that today.

It wasn't as if he was in a rush to build everything for the cabin, anyway. Jack had no idea what he'd do next, after making all of his own furniture. But he'd find some way to pass the time. Something to learn. Something to do. Some manner to push through the eternity of days God probably had planned for him. Days without his wife and children. Days to remember what he'd had, and what he'd lost.

For some reason, a vision of Elise, her mouth agape as she tried to understand why he hadn't notified anyone about seeing Cody, flashed through his mind. He wondered if she had children of her own. She appeared to be about his age, thirty-two, or a little younger. Late twenties or early thirties. And very attractive. He'd thought about *that* several times since yesterday too. Her heart-shaped mouth, dark chocolate eyes, flushed cheeks. Those rose-tinted cheeks, however, were probably more a result of her shock at learning he'd seen Cody the day before and hadn't called anyone.

There was something fascinating about a woman fiercely protecting her own.

He huffed out a breath. It didn't feel right thinking of her as attractive, or fascinating, or anything else. He'd loved Laney and didn't plan to care about anyone that way again. It hurt too much when God took her away. Even so, he couldn't stop glancing at the end of the trail and wondering if Elise would return.

Standing, he moved to the piece of mahogany already positioned for sanding on his saw-horses and prepared to uncover the beauty that would form the top of the dresser. Surely that would keep his mind off things he shouldn't be thinking.

He eyed the expensive piece of wood and wondered if he could do it justice. Typically, Jack didn't attempt anything he couldn't do well. Laney had often joked that she hadn't found an aspect of life where he didn't excel.

"You never saw me try to build furniture, did you?" he asked, though Laney certainly wasn't around to hear.

Jack's heart thudded in his chest. She'd have gotten a kick out of seeing him talk to himself, as well as watching him try to learn the mechanics of carpentry.

His father was a carpenter.

Elise's words trickled through his thoughts, reminding him of the boy who'd also lost his entire family.

Jack couldn't deny that he wanted to see Cody again. Nor could he deny that he wanted to see Elise again too. But he'd come here to get away from memories of the past, and a woman who cared so deeply, as well as a traumatized boy who desperately needed help, wouldn't do anything to keep those memories at bay. However, Jack's desire to reach out to a youngster struggling with the same grief that pierced his senses outweighed his instinct to protect his heart from more pain. He hadn't lied to Elise; he wanted—*needed*—to help the kid. But helping Cody would be near impossible if the boy wouldn't stick around long enough to interact with Jack.

He decided to replace thoughts of Elise and Cody with his concentration on the task at hand. Besides, the dresser would never get finished if he simply stood here looking at the woods all day watching for two people who might never return. He'd come here for peace, for solitude. He shouldn't want visitors.

He *shouldn't*.

Jack breathed in the distinctive scent of sawdust and turned his attention to the mahogany. Before coming here, he'd never thought about the process of building furniture, but since he started, he couldn't help but notice the parallels of creating a functional piece from mere wood and the Creation. God had crafted something beautiful out of nothing.

Jack's mind tripped over an idea, where a furniture builder spent hours upon hours generating a prized masterpiece, pouring his heart and soul into something that would stand the test of time, but the piece has no idea about its maker. The product of the creation has no appreciation for the love and care that went into its very existence.

Or does it?

As he gently sanded and slowly exposed the beauty of the wood grain, Jack honed the idea.

What would happen if, by the passing of the beloved piece of furniture from one generation to the next, a story unfolded about the love of that original creator displayed to each of his descendants, as long as the generations remembered him, appreciated him and made an effort to pass on his legacy? The depth of the love would only intensify and increase as generation after generation cared for its existence, protected it with their heart and soul.

How would audiences best relate to the scenario?

Jack played with thought after thought, idea after idea, until hours had passed. And then he realized he'd sanded the same spot for way too long, and the wood was no longer a piece of beauty. The marred blemish claimed all attention, extinguishing the perfection surrounding the scar.

Why were eyes always drawn to the flaw?

This would never be a piece to pass down to

generations. He'd ruined it. Because he hadn't been paying attention. Frustrated, he picked up the once expensive piece of wood, now worthless, and hurled it aside with gusto.

A movement to his right caught his attention, and he glanced up in time to see Cody retreating backward into the woods. How long had he been standing there while Jack lost himself in the plot? And in the pain of his past?

Jack had waited all day to see the boy, and now that he'd returned, he'd scared him away when he took his frustrations out on a piece of wood. "Cody?" Another urge to pray pushed forward, but he ignored it. "Why don't you come here and see what I'm doing? I'm building—attempting to build—furniture. Working on a dresser."

The boy wore a long-sleeved navy T-shirt with an old-fashioned red, white and blue Ford Mustang emblem on the front, jeans and tennis shoes, black with white soles and laces. His shoestrings weren't tied, and Jack hoped he didn't trip, but he also didn't want to say anything about it. He wouldn't do anything to threaten Cody's slow, timid progression across the yard.

The boy scanned the area, particularly the

sawhorses and tools, and then his attention moved to the discarded piece of wood. Veering to the left, he moved within a few feet of Jack in his quest to reach the mahogany. He was taller than Jack originally thought, thinner too, with long, lean fingers that cautiously reached toward the wood. He crouched beside the wide plank, then ran a palm reverently down its length.

Jack held his breath, waiting to see what the boy would do. Cody looked up, his eyes filled with pain, with a confusion Jack felt to his soul. Although he didn't speak, no words were necessary. And another whisper of an idea flitted across his brain. What if an entire movie followed the chronicles of an autistic boy, a brilliant, grief-ravaged boy who refused to share his thoughts with a world that didn't care.

But Jack cared.

And he felt the need to explain his actions to the distraught boy. "The wood is no longer any good. It's my fault. I sanded it too much."

Tears slid down Cody's cheeks.

Jack wanted to show him how badly he felt for scaring him. He moved toward the boy...

And messed up again.

In an effort to keep Jack at bay, Cody fell

backward, the white soles of his shoes flashing in the afternoon sunlight when he caught himself with his palms. Helpless to do anything but watch, Jack stood stone-still as Cody's behind hit the ground and he scooted away like a trapped animal attempting to flee.

Jack knew better than to make any type of move toward the kid, so he remained where he stood and made his voice as calm as possible. "I won't hurt you, Cody. I promise. I was just going to see if I could help."

Dark eyebrows dipped as Cody shuffled away, the heels of his shoes pushing against loose leaves and dirt in his retreat. He shook his head, a dark wave of bangs shifting with the move, while his attention darted from Jack to the discarded mahogany and back again.

And then his confused expression landed on Jack's thick beard.

Before Jack could say anything else, Cody scrambled to his feet and darted into the woods, disappearing down the path, while Jack ran a hand across the scruffy mess covering the lower half of his face.

Elise had made it about ten feet down the trail when she met Cody coming from the opposite direction. Conflicting emotions slammed her with his appearance. Happiness that he hadn't stayed gone long and found his way back without problem, and disappointment that she hadn't needed to go farther down the trail to find him, as in all the way to Jack's cabin.

She had no doubt that Cody had been to his favorite spot, but unfortunately, his time away hadn't produced a positive demeanor. His face was drawn and tense, eyes fixated beyond Elise as he brushed against her on the trail. "Cody?" She turned to follow him but stopped when her cell vibrated in her pocket.

Assuming she knew who was on the other end, she kept an eye on Cody as he headed toward his cabin and answered, "Hello?"

"He came back, but I scared him away."

The frustration in Jack's voice tugged at her heart. "What happened?"

A sharp intake of breath echoed through the line.

"Jack," she said, "how did you scare him away? I need to know so I can help him."

"At first, I thought it was the wood, but now I think it was the beard. Should've shaved it." His words were delivered as if talking more to himself than to Elise.

Her eyes slid closed, and she gripped the

phone, his behavior reminding her of so many conversations from the past, when she had to decipher what Anthony tried to say and fill in the missing pieces.

God, please, don't let me get sucked into trying to fix another man.

But even as she thought the words of the prayer, she found herself empathizing with the guy who had tried to help Cody and had come out short. "You said something about wood?"

"A piece of mahogany. I bought it for the top of the dresser, but then I got to sanding it and had my mind on—" another pause "—other things."

Her counselor's instinct pushed at her to ask about the "other things," but her experience with Anthony held those words in check. She didn't need to get too involved in Jack's world. Didn't want to find herself close enough to get hurt. She cleared her throat and prepared to tell him that she needed to see Cody, but his heavy sigh of discouragement forced her to continue the conversation until he found some form of comfort from his efforts to help her patient.

"You were sanding wood when he got there?" She visualized Cody happening upon Jack involved in the task and knew that he undoubtedly equated the man with some semblance of the carpenter who had raised him and loved him. But she didn't know why that would have upset Cody. "Did it seem to bother him?"

"I wasn't sanding when he got here. I'd gotten—" he sighed again, apparently searching for the right word "—irritated at myself for sanding the same spot too long and ruining the wood, and I was tossing it when Cody came through the woods."

Elise pictured the scene more clearly now. Cody had gone searching for Jack, but instead of finding the quiet, rugged carpenter he'd encountered the past two days, he'd happened upon an aggravated man who, from the sound of things, took his frustration out on a piece of mahogany.

As far as Elise knew, Cody hadn't been exposed to any form of abuse in his past, so she didn't think he'd been scared that Jack would hurt him. However, Jack's action triggered something, enough of a response that Cody had returned to Willow's Haven.

"Seeing me throw the wood bothered him, but I think it was the beard that caused him to leave." And again, he spoke more to himself than Elise.

She took a deep breath, let it out slowly, then said, "The beard hasn't bothered him before. Why do you think it did today?"

"I don't know, but I'm pretty good at reading people, or at least I was when I was working. And he was bothered by the beard."

When he was working. Elise wondered what the man did in the film industry, and how the guy could move to a cabin in the middle of nowhere without any apparent form of income. She started to ask, but then heard the whispers of warning in the back of her mind.

Getting too personal will make you care too much.

You have a patient with enough problems to keep you more than busy while you're here. Don't take on a man with issues too.

Protect your heart.

"Elise."

The way he said her name let her know he was fully involved in the conversation now, and she found herself anxious to hear more.

Protect your heart.

"Yes?"

"We can help him."

We? She closed her eyes, prayed for God to keep her from getting hurt…too much. Because she knew in her soul that Jack could hurt her, the same way she'd been hurt before.

A door slammed, and she opened her eyes to view Cody exiting his cabin, a big, tan canvas tote draped over his shoulder. He walked directly to her car, opened the passenger door and got in.

"I've got to go," she said. She heard his frustrated, "Goodbye, Elise," echo through the line and almost explained why she had to finish the conversation, but memories of the last man in her life gave her the courage to click the end button.

Plus, Cody sat waiting in her car.

Knowing he wouldn't use words to let her know what he wanted, she dashed to her cabin, grabbed her keys, her purse and the flash cards she used to communicate with him, and then hurried to the driver's side of the car.

He reached for the cards as soon as she climbed in, but Elise shook her head. "First I need to remind you that you shouldn't have left without letting someone know." She thumbed through the cards. "If you want to go for a hike, you show me this card." She held up the picture of a guy wearing a dark green shirt, jeans and hiking boots. Yesterday, she'd have said the guy in the photo looked rugged and outdoorsy. But then she'd met Jack. In his sawdust-coated flannel shirt, jeans and boots, he had rugged and outdoorsy mastered.

Cody tapped his fingers together at his chest, a signal of his anxiety, and Elise shook the image of Jack away and pointed to the hiking guy on the card. "So you show me this card the next time you want to go see— The next time you want to go for a walk in the woods. Understand?"

He bobbed his head and reached again for the cards. This time, Elise released the deck.

Cody, used to this routine, flipped through the stack so rapidly that the snapping cardboard sounded like popcorn within the confines of her Honda.

In spite of her uneasiness with the way her mind kept drifting back to Jack, she kept her voice low and controlled when she spoke. "Where do you want to go, Cody?"

In the two weeks since she'd arrived, she'd taken him to a few places, but never because he'd instigated the outing. This was new, and Elise felt a sense of accomplishment at the difference, even if initiated by his awkward interaction with Jack.

Cody stopped flicking the cards and then

pushed the deck toward her nose, his face full of seriousness as he awaited her response.

"The library?" They'd gone to the Claremont Public Library two days ago, and he'd checked out fifteen books, the maximum allotment. Each of them had to do with classic automobiles, rebuilding engines and carburetors and such. As far as Elise could tell, he'd reread a couple of them several times but hadn't made his way through the entire stack.

Unless he was reading them at night instead of sleeping.

She glanced at his eyes. No dark circles underneath, and his energy level hadn't appeared to falter during the day. Surely his cabin counselor would've noticed if he were staying up all hours in his room.

Or would he?

Elise pointed to the bulging canvas bag Cody had dropped at his feet. "I'm guessing those are your library books, then? You're wanting to exchange them for new books?"

Too impatient to find the *yes* card in the stack, Cody jerked his head up and down in a vigorous nod. Then he looked straight ahead, his legs bouncing and fingers drumming madly against his jeans.

Elise had become close to several of her

patients in the past, but there was something about Cody that nudged at her heart. His case file indicated he'd had a wonderful family, a picture-perfect life. And it'd all been taken away in the blink of an eye. Maybe *that* was why she was so drawn to him, and why he reminded her of the one aching desire that had been pushed aside during her marriage, because her husband wasn't emotionally ready.

She'd wanted children.

She *still* wanted children.

And Cody stirred that yearning more than any other child. She cared so much for him already, and she wanted him to have a chance to be a part of another wonderful family. He deserved that, and Elise wanted to make that happen by helping him overcome the barriers he'd set in place when his world had been upended.

She prayed this trip to the library would give her some insight as to what had bothered him at Jack's place. "Okay, then, to the library it is."

Twenty minutes later, Cody grabbed a plastic red book basket and handed a blue one to Elise. When she'd brought him here before, she'd selected the books that she knew would interest him based on his case file. But this time, Cody pulled her through the library and showcased his knowledge of computers and books, easily searching for his topic on the laptop at one of the information kiosks. He wasted no time writing the call numbers for the books he needed on the provided slips of scrap paper. Then he took off through the stacks at a speed that astounded Elise.

His autistic symptoms might most often be manifested in his knowledge of automobiles, as stated in his file, but the boy had skill in the library too. Each book had the same subject matter, with none of those selected having anything to do with classic cars.

One by one, as the librarian checked out all thirty books—since he put the maximum in each of their baskets—Elise smiled a little broader. Every book had to do with furniture. How to build furniture. How to select the best wood for building furniture. Tools needed for building furniture. Blueprints from craft masters to build one-of-a-kind pieces.

Everything to help him learn about what Jack did at his cabin.

By the time they returned to Willow's Haven, the sun had started dropping, and Elise wondered if he'd head to Jack's place to show him the books. "If you're planning another hike through the woods, you need to tell me, okay?"

Cody nodded once, then climbed out, not an easy feat, since he insisted on carrying all of the books himself, even though they hadn't fit into his tote. Thankfully, the librarian had provided him with a plastic bag to aid in the process.

To Elise's dismay, he turned away from the path leading to Jack's home and instead purposefully strode toward his cabin with the bags in tow.

"I guess you're going to read until dinner?" She attempted to mask her disappointment. "That's fine. But if you'd like for me to read some of the books to you, I'd be happy to."

He never looked back. Simply entered the cabin, where, Elise knew, he'd proceed to his bedroom and crack open the first book.

Sighing, she walked to her cabin and decided to spend the rest of her time this evening journaling the day's events in her ongoing file. She consulted with her colleagues daily on Cody's progress, or lack thereof, and they'd seen his recent wanderings as a positive response. She thought so too, and she now knew that he undoubtedly planned to visit Jack again. Which was good for Cody.

For Elise's heart, however, she wasn't so sure.

Chapter Three

Jack drizzled a generous portion of thick, golden honey across the bottom half of his biscuit, placed the lid back on and then enjoyed the sweet tastes melding on his tongue while watching the sun rise above the mountaintop. He began each morning at the cabin in this manner, sitting on the front porch and watching the yellow rays push through the tree branches and illuminate his property like long, golden fingers.

His mind drifted to yesterday, when Cody ran his fingers across the discarded wood with such reverence that Jack ached to know what transpired in the boy's mind. Why had he been so upset about the ruined mahogany? Surely it hadn't been the expense, because Jack suspected the boy had no idea about the cost. And the price didn't matter to Jack. He could build an entire cabin out of mahogany if he chose to. Not that he would. In spite of the ample funds in his bank account, he'd never been prone to live in excess. He couldn't justify living frivolously while so many barely scraped by.

But if it hadn't been the expense, what had bothered Cody so much about the wood? Jack glanced over his shoulder at the rejected piece, propped on the porch, a short distance away from the door. He hadn't had the heart to throw it in the burn pile, or even take it to the shed to use for a smaller piece of furniture. Because he hadn't wanted Cody to find it missing when he returned.

If he returned.

Jack was surprised at how quickly he'd developed such an attachment toward the boy. He'd vowed to never have kids again, because of the pain he'd experienced when he lost them, and in moving to the middle of nowhere, he had thought he'd never even be around children again.

But this was different. *Cody* was different. Not because Jack had changed his mind about wanting children again, but because he had to help this boy who'd been through the same horrific loss that Jack had experienced.

Yet he feared Cody might never come back.

And if Cody didn't return, neither would Elise.

Jack flinched, the awareness that he wanted to see a woman other than Laney stabbed a shard of guilt into his heart. He'd promised to love Laney forever, *till death do us part*.

Death *had* parted them, hadn't it?

Jack pushed aside the thoughts of Elise and the attraction that brushed the surface of their interactions regarding Cody. Because as much as he wanted to help the child, he also wanted to see Elise.

But he didn't *want* to want to see her.

He ran his palm across his slick chin. It'd felt rather nice to get rid of the heavy mass, almost liberating. But it also gave him the sense of being exposed, so that when he did encounter people, they'd see more, know more, about his pain.

However, as much as that prospect bothered him, the fact that his facial hair may have deterred the boy from feeling comfortable around him caused Jack to put his razor to good use. If Cody came back today, he'd make a better effort at gaining his trust.

He looked again to the broken area in his border of trees, the narrow path that'd brought his only two visitors since he'd arrived here. As he watched, the sun rose a little higher, showcasing the very spot where they'd appeared.

And then Jack saw him, ambling out of the path with awkwardness to his steps, as though he were off balance.

"Cody." Careful not to jump up from where he sat on the porch, Jack maintained his composure and kept his voice steady. "Hey, I hoped you'd come back."

His gait a little stilted and his pace slow and guarded, Cody eased toward the cabin as though he didn't want to rush this encounter. Or as though preparing to bolt the way he did yesterday.

As he neared, he tilted his head, the way Jack had seen him do before, and a large chunk of dark brown hair fell across his right eye with the gesture. Today's shirt was similar to yesterday's, except it was forest green and had a photo of a '67 Chevelle on the chest. And like before, he wore dark jeans and those black-and-white tennis shoes, laces untied.

He frowned and stared at Jack's face, specifically his chin.

Jack ran his hand across the skin. "It's still me, just no beard." He thought Cody's head moved a fraction in a slight nod. Maybe the boy would stick around a little longer this time. Then Jack's attention shifted to the cream-colored tote hanging from Cody's right arm and the green plastic bag on the other. They sagged from heavy contents, and Cody clasped his hands together to brace his arms from the weight.

"What have you got there?" Jack pointed to the bulging bags.

But Cody wasn't paying attention to his baggage. Instead, he focused on Jack's plate of biscuits.

"Cody?" Elise called his name breathlessly as she emerged from the trail. Jack and the boy both turned toward the woman holding a hand to her chest as she moved toward them. Her cheeks were flushed, and her hair, unlike the last time he'd seen her, wasn't captured in a ponytail but fell in long, dark waves around her shoulders, the way it'd been when he saw her crying in the woods. Jack made a mental note to eventually learn what made her cry that day, but now wasn't the time. Judging from her appearance, she'd started the morning by learning her patient had, once again, gone AWOL.

She looked as though she'd yanked on the first clothes she could find, which happened to be an oversize white T-shirt with a disgruntled bulldog in the center and the caption Got Coffee? at the top, jeans that had a rip above the left knee and hiking boots.

Jack thought the sunrise would be the prettiest thing he'd see this morning. He'd been wrong. There was something about a woman early in the day, before she looked so put together and when she had that vulnerable, just-woke-up appeal, that grabbed his heart and held it captive.

The way Elise held it captive now.

It'd been a long time, two years, since he'd seen a woman like this, her cheeks glowing from embarrassment that he'd caught her unprepared for the day. His first thought was that he'd like to share a cup of coffee with a woman like that. His second thought was that he didn't want to give his heart to a woman again. And his third thought…

She looked at him as though she had no idea who he was.

"Elise?" He'd been so long without regular human interaction that his voice still sounded odd to his own ears. Rough and raspy. Still, he liked the way it felt when he said her name.

Her chin dropped, one eyebrow lifted and she whispered, "Jack?"

He'd thought she couldn't look cuter than she had disheveled and emerging from the woods at barely past seven in the morning. But he'd thought wrong. Her confused expression added another layer of vulnerability. She'd look incredible on film.

Jack pushed the reminder of his previous life away and focused instead on the woman before him. "Yeah, it's me," he said, managing a smile for his guests.

"Wow."

He could tell by the way her cheeks flushed even more that she hadn't meant to release the whispered word and, truthfully, he experienced a little embarrassment—or something—of his own, because it didn't appear to be a term of surprise that he'd shaved, but a whisper of appreciation. And it ebbed through him much like those sun rays eased through the trees, warming him, reminding him of the way it felt to be seen as a man by a beautiful woman.

Cody pointed to the plate and broke the charged tension that'd caught Jack by surprise.

Jack cleared his throat and did his best not to stare at the woman now walking toward his porch. Instead, he focused on the boy, standing very near now, and still pointing at the plate filled with biscuits.

"You want some?" he asked.

Another slight nod, and then Cody dropped the heavy bags to the ground and sat on the middle step.

"Cody's cabin counselor called me when he didn't show up at the dining cabin for breakfast. He left with the group but must have taken a detour on the way. I figured he might have come here." Elise pushed a heavy wave of hair away from her face as she spoke. "Cody, I asked you to tell an adult when you want to leave Willow's Haven. Remember?"

Cody nodded and frowned.

"Okay. Let's make sure to do that next time. Understand?"

Another nod, and then Cody returned his attention to the plate of biscuits and pointed again.

Elise laughed softly. "I'm sure he's hungry, if you have enough."

"I've got plenty." Jack was glad he'd fixed the large can of biscuits. "Hang on, I'll get some more from inside." Then he wondered whether they'd also want to eat on the porch, the way he'd done since he moved in. "Or would y'all rather come in to eat? I don't have a kitchen table yet. I haven't gotten that far in my furniture building. But we could eat…" He didn't exactly know where they'd eat. There wasn't much in the cabin yet beyond a desk, a few chairs and a mattress.

"Out here is fine." Elise still stared at his face. "I— You look so different."

And that was all it took for that raw, exposed feeling to take over and for him to wonder how much she saw. He could tell by the expression on her face—and by the one-word exclamation earlier—that she didn't mind the way he looked. But could she see more than mere appearance? Like how he felt empty without the family that completed him? Or how he blamed God for taking everything he loved away, so much that he refused to make another film to glorify a Creator who hadn't cared?

Instead of responding, he stood and started inside. "I'll get more." Then he stopped at the door. "I have coffee, if you want some. And milk for you, Cody, if you like."

"Coffee is fine," she said. "I don't need anything in it, though. And Cody loves milk."

Thankful that he at least had some dishes, and also grateful for the supply of groceries he'd gathered from Stockville last week, Jack left them on the porch to gather the breakfast items. He'd bought an abundance of food because he didn't plan to go into town more than a couple times per month. And he'd chosen Stockville, a city a little farther away, for his shopping to limit his exposure and noticeability to the folks who'd most likely show up for a visit.

Little did he know Cody would find him by merely walking through the woods.

Jack didn't need to get wrapped up in the desires of a boy JJ's age, didn't need to have visitors or feed them when they showed up at his door. But Cody wasn't just "some boy." He'd been through more than any other kid Jack had known, losing his parents, his entire family. The same way Jack lost his. How could he *not* try to help the child?

He poured the coffee and milk and brought them out to find Elise standing so close to the entrance that he nearly hit her with the door.

She took a step back, but not far enough that he didn't catch her citrusy scent. And he found himself enjoying it much more than the yeasty smell of the biscuits and crisp aroma of coffee that filled the kitchen.

"I thought you might need help carrying things out, but I didn't want to come in without asking." She looked at him shyly and, though she didn't have on an ounce of makeup, her dark eyes couldn't have been prettier amid that sea of brown lashes.

Jack didn't like the way that he noticed her eyes, or the way she smelled, or anything else. He'd never wanted to notice another woman that way, never wanted any other woman but his wife. And he didn't want to betray Laney's memory. But Elise was clearly here for Cody, not Jack, and in order to help the boy, he'd undoubtedly spend time with the woman who had the same goal. Helping the child. Nothing more, nothing less.

She inched away from him. "I don't have to help if you'd rather I not go in."

Jack had never been rude, and he wouldn't start now. He eased the door open wider. "No, that'd be great. The biscuits are on the stove." Then he felt the need to apologize. "And ignore the fact that there isn't much in there yet. Like I said, I'm still working on the furniture."

She gave him a soft smile and stepped inside while he placed her coffee mug on the top step near his own and then handed Cody the glass of milk.

Cody took a big sip, keeping his mouth firmly against the cup while he gulped several swallows, and then placed the cup beside him on the middle step. He had a milk mustache that Jack might have mentioned, but he didn't want to do anything that would cause the boy to be embarrassed. Or to leave. And he realized that he'd been preparing for this moment, waiting for it, since Cody left yesterday. Not only the chance to try to help the boy, but also the chance to spend time with the pretty therapist exiting his cabin with the remainder of the biscuits.

How he ached for a woman's touch, not merely her physical touch, but for her touch in his home. Just a quick glance around his Spartan surroundings revealed the absence—the need—of a feminine presence. But he couldn't think about that now. He had a mission. To help a little boy.

And if that meant spending time with this attractive lady, he would.

"You'd already buttered them, right?" she asked, and Jack pushed those wayward thoughts aside.

He nodded. "Yeah, and I hope y'all like butter. I'm kind of partial to it."

"I can see that." The right corner of her mouth lifted as she moved to the top step and then pulled the lower plate out from under the one that held the remaining six biscuits. Jack had taken two earlier and still had one on his plate. "I love butter, and I'm pretty sure Cody does too."

She put three of the biscuits on a plate and handed them to Cody. "That about right for you, Cody?"

He didn't answer but stared at the biscuits, and she must have taken that as a *yes*, because she then turned to Jack. "You want another one, or two?"

"One," he said, finding it oddly comforting to sit beside her on the porch and have her serve him a biscuit, as if this were something natural. And as if he hadn't been eating all of his meals alone for as long as he could remember.

Cody hadn't touched his biscuits but instead looked to Elise as though waiting for something. Jack watched as she gave the boy a little smile.

"Would you like to say grace for us?" she asked Jack.

His skin prickled, and he had the sudden recollection of AmyJo and Sadie singing their prayer at the kitchen table. "You can." He couldn't control the gruffness of his tone induced by the bittersweet memory.

Her mouth slid to the side, eyebrows dipped in concern, but then she bowed her head. "Dear God, thank You for letting me find Cody this morning, and thank You for Jack's willingness to share his meal. Bless this food, Lord, and bless our day. In Your Son's name, amen."

Apparently, the word *amen* held the same connotation as *ready-set-go* for Cody, because he scooped up a biscuit the moment she finished and nearly ate half of it in one bite. His mouth worked vigorously as he chewed, and he grabbed his glass of milk and gulped more to get it down.

"Hey now, slugger—" Jack patted Cody's knee "—slow down, or you'll get choked."

Elise nibbled on her biscuit but laughed as she chewed. "He's right, Cody. Take your time." She spotted the jar Jack had tucked behind the porch post. "Is that honey?"

Jack had already coated his first two biscuits, but he should've thought to offer some to his guests. He reached for the jar. "You'll have to forgive me. I'm...not used to having company."

She took the honey, waited a beat, then asked, "And you weren't really planning on having anyone here at all, were you?" The question begged for an answer that elaborated on his reasons for setting up his home in the middle of nowhere, escaping civilization and everything it entailed, all of the pain it instilled, but Jack wasn't ready to explain. Didn't know if he'd ever be ready. He'd already told her more than he'd planned.

So he simply said, "No, I wasn't," and when he saw Cody frown, he added, "But it's okay."

The boy didn't smile, but the frown lifted into the flat line that he often displayed when he appeared to tighten every muscle in his face in an effort to control...something. Maybe that kept him from speaking when he wasn't ready to talk yet. Or maybe that was the way he hid his own emotions. Rather than build a cabin in the woods, he built a fortress around his words and protected them with a vengeance.

Suddenly, Cody pointed toward the jar Elise now held in her hand.

"You want some too, Cody?" she asked with a smile. When he held his plate toward her, she lifted the top off one of his remaining biscuits and poured the honey in the center. "See what you think."

The boy took a big bite and hummed so deeply it sounded like a growl.

Elise's eyes lit up. "That good, huh?" She drizzled the honey on her two biscuits and grinned when Cody held his plate toward her for more. She obliged him by covering the other biscuit with honey and then told Jack, "I hope you have more inside, because we're making a huge dent in your stash."

"I bought a few jars when I went to the store last week, so I'm good." He'd thought it would last him a while, but if he had more morning visits from Elise and Cody, that might not be the case, because Cody was again motioning for more of the sweet substance, and still humming.

"It's delicious." She took another bite. "Is it local?"

"Yeah, I bought it in Stockville. The woman at the grocery had it for sale near the counter and said she gets it from a beekeeper that lives nearby." He ate more of his biscuit and tried to recall the last time he'd had casual conversation while sharing a meal. He couldn't. And the realization not only made him grateful for this time, but sorrowful that he'd been without anything like it for so long.

He truly missed his family.

"That'll keep you from getting sick, you know." She grinned as Cody ran a finger through some of the honey that had escaped his biscuits and pooled on his plate. He popped it in his mouth and hummed even louder.

"Honey will keep me from getting sick?" Jack took another bite.

She nodded as she sipped her coffee. "That's what my grandmother always said. She put a spoonful in her coffee each morning to help with colds and allergies." She shrugged, took another bite of biscuit. "I have no idea whether it actually works, or if it's an old wives' tale, but that's the story. Something about taking in the local pollen to build up your immunity."

Jack had never heard anything like that, but he knew that people from the South had their own way of looking at things, their old-fashioned remedies that often proved to be true. He'd stayed in a small town near Birmingham a few years ago when filming *Jacob's Dream* and had fallen in love with the easy lifestyle, the moderate climate and the charm and grace of Southerners in general. It'd been part of the reason he'd looked for something in this location when he'd decided to retreat from the world, the beauty of the place, rather than the people. He hadn't planned on getting all that close to the community.

But here he was, undeniably getting close to these two.

Cody held up his palms, and Jack saw that, while all of his biscuits and the entire glass of milk were gone, his hands were shiny from honey, particularly his fingers, since he'd slid them all over the plate in an effort to eat every drop.

"Hang on," Jack said. "I'll get something to clean that up."

He went inside, got a dishcloth and wet it with warm water, then returned to the porch. "Wipe them with this." He handed the cloth over and watched as Cody meticulously worked it over his palms and then in around each finger. After he finished, he handed it to Elise, who did the same and then passed it to Jack, who followed suit.

Once her hands were clean, Elise gathered

the plates while Jack scooped up the cups and honey, and then they started inside while Cody moved toward the bags he'd dropped earlier.

She paused at the door. "We'll be right back, Cody. Don't leave me again, okay?"

Naturally, he didn't answer, and she released a light sigh as she and Jack carried the things inside.

"He liked the biscuits." Elise rinsed the plates and stacked them in the sink. "I haven't heard him hum like that before." She smiled. "That's the first sound he's made at all since I started working with him."

"But you said he can communicate." Jack remembered her mentioning it on the first day.

Her shoulders rose and fell in a small shrug. "He could before the accident."

"And now he doesn't." Jack's empathy toward the boy intensified. Yes, Jack had lost his family too, but he'd only withdrawn from society. Cody had withdrawn from everything.

"Now he doesn't," she repeated softly.

"Without speaking, I'm guessing the chances for an autistic boy to be adopted are slim to nil," Jack deduced, and he sensed the need to pray for the boy. If only he still believed God would answer his prayers.

Elise didn't answer, but her silence said everything. The boy needed to communicate in order to stand a chance at a family wanting to adopt him.

Pondering Cody's situation and what he could do to help, Jack put the honey in the cabinet, then moved to the sink and placed the cups beside the stacked plates while carefully maintaining his distance from the woman in his kitchen. The cabin wasn't small, but the room seemed to shrink with Elise's presence. He didn't want to stand too close, didn't want to be too close. But he also needed her to understand that he didn't want to stop seeing Cody. Today was the first day Jack had felt alive in a very long time.

"I'm glad he came back today. I think it's good for him, to come here."

"I believe it is too." She'd started walking toward the door but stopped and peered out his front window to see Cody. "And I think I figured out why he was so bothered by the wood yesterday, or rather, I figured it out after discussing his behavior with my colleagues."

"Why?" Jack still thought the beard had bothered him, but whatever unsettled the boy had started when he saw the marred mahogany.

"That wood was perfect, something useful

and wanted, and then, because of what happened to it, it wasn't useful anymore." She shook her head as she continued staring out the window at the boy. "Autism is something that some people simply can't handle."

"Or think they can't handle." Jack's throat tightened, fists clenched on their own accord.

"The goal at Willow's Haven is to find the perfect family for Cody, one that will love him for who he is and not what they believe he should be." She glanced at Jack, then added, "But Cody seems to be making progress toward that direction now."

"With me?" He wanted to hear her say it, even though he was fairly certain he knew the answer.

"Yes, with you." She continued toward the door. "Did you see what he brought in the bags?"

"No, I didn't." Jack had noticed the heavy things, but he hadn't thought the contents had anything to do with him.

She opened the door and they found Cody withdrawing the last of a stack of books from the canvas tote. Another stack, presumably from the green bag, sat nearby. "Well, it looks like he's ready to show you."

Jack eyed the titles and then watched as

Cody, sitting on the ground with the books surrounding him and flipped open to various pages, looked up with an expression of what could only be described as…hope.

He stepped closer and saw that each opened page had diagrams and information on building furniture. More specifically, on ways to salvage wood. Jack's heart thudded solidly in his chest, and he tilted his head toward the discarded piece of mahogany propped against the side of the porch. "Looks like somebody's ready to get to work," he said, and then he saw the second look of hope, this time…from Elise.

In the two weeks since she'd started working with Cody, Elise had never seen him as energized as he was now, poring over diagrams of furniture with Jack. No, he wasn't speaking, but the nonverbal communication had escalated. He tapped the pictures on the pages and nodded excitedly when Jack talked about what they could do to repair that ruined piece of wood. Right now, in fact, as Jack lifted the mahogany slab and described how they could use something called a planer to fix the marred area, Cody clapped. Not the tapping of fingers at his chest that he often did when bored or confused or anxious, but an honest-to-goodness happy clap.

The guy had no idea how much progress Cody had made in a single day, but Elise did, and it warmed her heart, toward the boy she already cared so much about and toward the reclusive man lowering his own barriers against the world to help the child.

"Well, okay, then. If that's what we need, I'll get one." Jack gave Cody a smile that tugged at Elise's chest, and then he looked at her and— Maybe she imagined it, but the smile seemed to hitch a little higher.

Maintaining a hold on her undeniable attraction would've been tough when he was rough-mountain-man Jack; with clean-shaven-and-*GQ*-model-worthy Jack, it was going to be near impossible.

However, she couldn't deny that there was something *off* with a guy who voluntarily chose to live in total solitude, without a neighbor and with no semblance of community whatsoever.

This was the kind of guy she'd promised never to get involved with again. *This* was the kind of guy who could destroy what was left of her heart.

And yet Cody's progress had been nonexistent before he met Jack. No way could she put a halt to that.

"You want anything from inside?" He'd stopped at the door and waited for her answer. "Something to drink? I have lemonade and tea."

"Lemonade would be great." And it would help the fact that her mouth went desert dry whenever he grinned at Cody, flexed his abundance of muscles lifting a piece of lumber… or locked eyes with her.

Elise pushed the realization out of her thoughts, and as she moved from the porch steps to sit beside Cody, his demeanor didn't change. He remained eager and alert, and even showed her a photo of a large piece of machinery on one of the pages of a book.

"Is that what y'all need to fix the wood?"

He nodded and then smiled. At Elise. She had prayed repeatedly over the past two weeks to see a sign of happiness from Cody. To see that smile.

Thank You, God.

Jack exited the cabin, his cell phone in one hand and a glass of lemonade in the other. Talking into the phone, he held the glass toward Elise. She took it and tried to ignore the electric jolt that shimmied up her arm when his fingers brushed against hers. Thankfully, Jack seemed too into his conversation to notice. She had to get a grip on this attraction before he caught on.

"My reception isn't that great in some spots here." He took a few steps away toward the open clearing and then said, "Yes, that's what we want, and I do need delivery." He frowned. "Is that the quickest you can get it here? I was hoping for this afternoon… I see. Yeah, if you've got to have it shipped in, I guess that'll do." He disconnected, then turned toward Cody and Elise sitting on the ground near the splayed books. "We can't get the planer before tomorrow," he said to Cody, "but I still need to sand the drawer fronts. If you'd like to help, we can do that today."

Cody scrambled to his feet, dusted the dirt off his jeans and slapped his hands together.

"I think he's ready to work." Elise didn't have a chance to stand before Jack held his hand toward her.

"Here, let me help."

She slid her hand in his, the warmth of his palm enveloping her as he easily assisted her up. "Thanks."

He stood near, very near, and he didn't make an effort to move away. Or release her hand.

Elise's breathing hitched, and she prayed he didn't notice. Standing this close, she observed tiny flecks of gold within his green eyes. It'd be easy to lose yourself in those eyes, especially when he examined Elise with the same intensity as she studied him.

Her cheeks tingled, and she had no doubt they'd tinged red. But before she could speak and break the moment, he did.

"You're so...different."

Not what she expected. Different from what? Or who? She started to ask, but a loud knock behind them caused them to turn and see Cody, slapping his palm against one of the drawer fronts Jack had placed on a worktable nearby.

Jack released her hand, shook his head as though frustrated with something, or maybe with himself, then left her and strode toward Cody. "Let me show you what we need to do, JJ."

Cody tilted his head, brow furrowed.

Elise, however, asked the question that Cody couldn't. "JJ?"

All color drained from Jack's face. "Cody," he quickly corrected. "Let me show you what we need to do, *Cody*." He handed the boy a sanding block, and he took it, all confusion disappearing from his features. The boy was too eager to help Jack with the furniture to concern himself with the fact that he'd been called the wrong name.

But Elise *was* concerned. She needed Jack to get through to Cody, but Jack, like every other man in her life, had something going on in his world, something that needed mending.

There are some things you simply can't fix, Elise. Some people are too broken, and there's nothing you can do about it.

Her oldest brother's words, spoken at Anthony's funeral, haunted her now. She couldn't go through that again.

Jack gently moved the sanding block in a circular motion and coached Cody as he did the same on the adjacent drawer. He glanced up to catch Elise staring at him, lost in the painful memory and not knowing how to keep the past from repeating itself.

She should leave. Take Cody and go, right here, right now. He said she was different, but Elise had no idea how. He called Cody another name, someone named JJ. Warning bells—no, warning *blasts*—resounded through her head, until she felt her pulse in her ears. She moistened her lips, prepared to tell Cody that they needed to go.

"You want to help?" Jack held another sanding block toward Elise. "We have plenty of drawer fronts to do, and then we can move on to the frame."

Cody paused from sanding, looked up and smiled. Again. Another smile that she'd prayed for. His only progress had occurred because of Jack.

She had no choice. "Sure."

Chapter Four

Typically, Jack put his cell phone on silent when he slept, but evidently he'd forgotten when he'd climbed in bed, because it blared to life well before sunup. No one called him in the middle of the night. Everyone at the studio knew better than to disturb his family when they were resting.

His mind jolted from the old train of thought. He had no family to disturb, not anymore. Still, no one would call at this time of night unless it were an emergency.

His first thought went to his parents. He hadn't spoken to them in at least a month, and they'd sounded fine when they called from their summer house in the Keys. But maybe something had happened to his mom or dad. Or his sister? It'd been even longer since he'd spoken to Sarah. They hadn't had much to talk about since the plane crash, nothing in common anymore. She still had her husband, two sons and three daughters consuming her world. And Jack couldn't handle hearing about her happy, busy family. Plus, Sarah seemed uncomfortable talking about her picture-perfect life when she knew the best part of his ended when that plane went down.

But something could've happened with Sarah. Maybe the kids *weren't* okay. And now she needed him the way he'd needed her two years ago.

He squinted at the display on the phone. No Caller ID flashed back. Strange. A family member's contact info should show up. Brow furrowed, he punched the send button and answered, "Jack Simon."

"So now I know what to do to get in touch with you." The raspy, commanding tone left no doubt that the great Roland Mooreland himself had decided the best way to deal with his director gone rogue was to contact Jack personally.

He sat up in bed, rubbed his eyes and prepared for what was certain to be an uncomfortable conversation. "Good morning,

Roland. You didn't want to let Vincent convey your message?"

"Why would I do that? Based on what I've heard from your agent, you haven't been taking his calls and therefore haven't *received* any of my messages." Roland coughed violently into the phone, then followed it with a long slurp of what Jack suspected was his trademark bitter black coffee.

"I haven't taken anyone's calls." Jack flipped the switch on the bedside lamp and squinted through the bright assault of illumination. "I'd assumed that would've been expected, since I told Vincent I wouldn't have anything else to do with the film."

"Which is why we pushed the release back a year, to give you time to—" another slurp of coffee "—do what you had to do in order to get your life on track after…" He hesitated, clearly at a loss for how to throw the truth into a sentence.

Jack didn't have any trouble, however, filling in the blank. "After God took my entire family on the night of my last premiere?"

A tense silence echoed through the line, and Jack could almost see the wheels of Roland's mind churning. Should he address the fact that his director blamed God for everything he'd lost? Did he dare use the everything-happens-for-a-reason line that most people chose when talking to Jack since that day? Because he wouldn't have any part of that. What *reason* could explain him losing his entire family?

As he suspected, Roland chose to forego any type of explanation and forged straight ahead with his most prominent need, getting Jack to promote the film.

"Listen, Jack, *Finding Home* should've released last fall, but we got away with holding it over a year because of—" he coughed "—because of what happened last time. The studio understood that you needed a break. But there are a lot of folk counting on this film. The public latched onto *Jacob's Dream* and *The Journey.* You know how important it is to capitalize on the momentum of two number-one box office hits."

Jack waited while Roland drank more coffee and held on for input from his director.

Jack said nothing.

Roland grumbled something under his breath, then continued, "You've become known as the 'faith director,' the guy who can bring God to theaters in a big way. Thanks to you, Damascus Entertainment is finally competing with the secular market, and Christians worldwide are anxious for this new film. They've been waiting for it for two long years, and we aren't going to make them wait any longer, Jack."

"Sounds like you've made up your mind, Roland. Don't know why you're calling me at—" he eyed the clock "—four in the morning."

"It's 2:00 a.m. in LA," Roland said. "Figured I'd catch you before you start that hideous early morning run ritual. And I thought if I called at an odd enough hour, you'd consider the possibility of a family emergency and pick up the line."

Jack had to hand it to him; the guy was smart. Then again, most studio execs were. But Roland went above the typical intelligence of the big players in LA, primarily because he wasn't merely working for himself. He considered Christians as a whole and the way they benefited from the product he put on the market. And he knew *Finding Home* wouldn't be as successful as Jack's previous films without the director's promotion.

But Jack didn't want to promote a film for God. Didn't want to do anything for Him. He certainly hadn't done anything for Jack.

"We need you on board." Roland's authoritative tone said he wouldn't back down.

Neither would Jack. "That's not happening, Roland, and I'm pretty sure you knew that when you called." He sat up, swung his feet off the side of the bed and sighed heavily as he ran a frustrated hand over his stubble. This conversation was going south fast.

An onslaught of nonstop coughing rumbled through the line, undoubtedly triggered by Jack's refusal. Guilt nudged Jack's heart. He liked Roland and had always appreciated the fact that he stood for something he believed in within an industry that typically cared only about the take at the box office. And Jack felt sorry for him. The mighty exec had been a heavy smoker in his youth and currently battled emphysema as a result of the teenage vice.

"Roland, have you got your oxygen handy?"

"Don't you worry about me and my lungs. I've got this under control. What I need you to worry about are the appearances Marketing and PR has scheduled for you." He rattled through a clearing of his throat. "Screening is set for the day after Thanksgiving, then three weeks of talk shows and print interviews, with the official release, as you know, on Christmas."

Christmastime and Easter, the two best dates of the year for releasing a Christian film, and Jack knew Roland would spare no expense in the press junket. "Sounds like a good press run," he said. "But you'll have to set it up without me. Book the cast…that should satisfy the public."

"That won't suffice, Jack, and you know it. Now, I'm going to tell our PR team to book your appearances, and you're going."

Jack clenched his jaw, counted to five and then answered, "I'm not, Roland. Now, I made a good film for you. It was the best I could do, and the public will love it. But I'm not making any more, and I'm *not* promoting it."

"The public needs to *know* that it's the best you could do, and they need to hear that from *you*. Not the cast. Not me. Not our PR team. They trust *you* to give them a God-focused film, something that will make them cry, laugh, cheer…and pray. You do that, Jack, every time, and they want to know that you'll do it again with *Finding Home*."

Jack had heard this before, many times, and he knew better than to try to stop Roland while he was on a roll, so he took a deep breath and braced for the rest.

Roland didn't miss a beat. "We need the

public behind this film before it even hits the screen. We need their faith, their prayers, pushing this to be the most popular movie in the world. Think of the lives we can touch. Don't you remember the photos and videos of people leaving the theaters after *The Journey* and *Jacob's Dream*? They were gathering in huddles right then and there and praying, Jack. And this movie is even stronger, will produce even more of a spiritual journey for everyone who sees it. How can you *not* want to promote it?"

Jack pressed his fingers against his forehead, pushed them outward to fend off the throbbing in his temples. "How can I promote something that I no longer believe? Tell me that, Roland."

Roland hissed out a thick breath. "You're contractually obligated, Jack. You know I don't want to go that route, but I will. We've already pushed the release back twelve months. We aren't going to lose any more time, and we aren't releasing this film without director backing."

"Are you honestly going to sue me? Is that what you're saying?"

"Listen, Jack. I like you. I've always liked you. You're the best director in the business if you ask me, but I'm not going to let this film get any less credit than it deserves, and without your endorsement, it won't stand a chance against the heavy hitters that weekend." He hardened his tone. "So yeah, I'll do whatever it takes to make you fulfill your end of the deal."

The throbbing pulsed mercilessly against his temples. Jack pressed against the ache and tried to remember if he'd bought any aspirin. "Roland, you don't want to do that."

"You're right, Jack, I don't. But I will. The first thing on your junket is the day after Thanksgiving, the screening in LA. You can be there, or you can expect to hear from the studio's attorney."

The line clicked as Roland disconnected. Jack growled his frustration, tossed the phone on the bed and searched for his running clothes. No, it wasn't daylight yet, but he needed to burn off some steam, and the prospect of getting more sleep was about as likely as the prospect of fulfilling his duties in Roland's press junket.

Not happening.

Elise hardly slept. The past two days had thrown her world off-kilter, and her mind wouldn't stop replaying the most surprising— and somewhat disturbing—moments. Finding Jack, a reclusive loner she still only knew by first name, living in the woods. Seeing Cody start easing out of his shell because of Jack. Feeling an attraction toward a guy who exuded every characteristic of the type of man she'd promised to avoid forever.

What made Cody relate to this guy?

Why did Jack see her as different?

Who was JJ?

For that matter, who was *Jack*?

She'd woken at five thirty, or more accurately, that was when she decided to get out of the bed and give up on any additional sleep. By six thirty, she'd already showered, dried her hair and gotten dressed. Breakfast would be served promptly at seven, when she'd meet up with Cody and begin their day, probably by heading to Jack's place as soon as they finished eating so they could find out what this "planer" thing could do to repair the wood.

She should tell Cody they couldn't go. Because every way she played out how this scenario with the recluse might end, there was one fundamental truth that could not be denied: she wouldn't be able to fix a broken man.

And Jack was most definitely broken.

She examined her reflection in the bathroom mirror as she brushed her hair and pulled it into a high ponytail. Gray shadows tinted the skin beneath each eye, a sure sign that she'd tossed and turned most of the night. She unzipped her makeup bag and withdrew a stick of concealer, swiped it over each side and then smoothed it in. After performing a quick scan of the other contents in the bag, she selected a shimmery rose-tinted gloss and skimmed it over her lips.

Another look in the mirror showed a lady who hadn't cared about wearing makeup since she'd arrived at Willow's Haven but suddenly found the need to hide her dark circles and draw attention to her lips.

"God help me."

She reached for a tissue to wipe the gloss away but stopped when an urgent knock sounded from the cabin door. The impatient rattle left no doubt who she'd find on the other side.

When she opened the door, her suspicion rang true.

Cody shifted so quickly from foot to foot that he appeared to be jogging in place. His fingers tapped together at his chest, but the hiking flash card kept his fingertips from touching and snapped with each beat of his hands.

Resolved that her workday would start a little earlier than she'd anticipated, she asked quietly, "Cody, is everything okay?"

He stopped the tapping, turned the card to make certain Elise saw the picture and then pointed to the mountain man.

As much as she wasn't thrilled about Jack proving to be the best means of helping Cody, she acknowledged her patient's progress. Instead of barging into the woods on his own, he'd taken the time to inform her of his plan and include her in his journey.

Definitely a step in the right direction.

"Thank you for telling me that you want to go see Jack." While she spoke, several boys and girls as well as cabin counselors passed her front porch heading toward the dining cabin.

Dylan Evans, Brodie and Savvy's fifteen-year-old son, stopped on his way. He wore a Claremont football jersey and khakis, game day attire for the junior varsity team and a stark contrast to Cody's choice of clothing, yet another classic car T-shirt paired with dark jeans.

Even the way Cody dressed served as a reminder that things were different in his world.

"Hey, Ms. Elise. Hey, Cody. Y'all coming to breakfast?"

Cody didn't acknowledge he'd heard Dylan's question, didn't even turn to see who had spoken. Thankfully, Dylan had become familiar with Cody's lack of communication and didn't seem bothered by the snub.

"We'll see." She knew better than to promise they would go, because she suspected eating was the last thing on Cody's mind.

"Okay, but they're fixing banana pancakes, if you change your mind." Dylan turned and sprinted to catch up with some of the teen boys from the next cabin. He was a great kid, energetic and genuinely happy. His birth mother, Willow, had passed away a couple of years ago, and Brodie and Savvy had adopted him and his two sisters. At one of the devotions last week, he explained how Willow's Haven was named after his mom and had been formed so more kids could find a new home, like he and his little sisters had found with Brodie and Savvy.

Elise wanted Cody to have a chance at a family like that. She'd worked with a few autistic children who had been adopted, but none of them had gone through the upheaval Cody had experienced. Based on his case file, he'd been very communicative and on track to function independently in society as an adult. He'd even been mainstreamed into the public school system last year, but since the accident occurred merely a week before this school year began, he hadn't even started yet.

Each morning, when Dylan and all the other kids at Willow's Haven were picked up by the school bus, Elise was reminded of yet another thing on the long list of goals she had for her patient, getting him back to school.

But Cody was nowhere near ready. However, he *had* started making progress, because of the handsome recluse at the end of the trail.

As if knowing where her thoughts had headed, Cody huffed out a thick breath and slapped the hiking card.

Elise nodded, acknowledging the request. "I know you want to go, but wouldn't you like to have breakfast first? They should begin serving in a few minutes. Banana pancakes sound great to me."

His lower lip rolled in, head shook emphatically. For a moment, she thought he might say—or even yell—his refusal, but instead he pushed the hiking card so close to her face that it nearly touched the tip of her nose.

Elise peered over the card expecting to see frustration or defiance that she'd even suggested they wait until after the meal, but instead she found sadness. Longing. Pleading.

He *needed* to see Jack.

She closed the door and prayed that she could keep herself from needing the same thing. Why did she feel so compelled to fix broken men?

Elise took a deep breath, let it out and mentally tightened the lock on her heart. She *would* keep this relationship with Jack professional. She had to. Otherwise she might not survive the fallout. "Okay, let's go."

His mouth stretched outward, and for a moment she thought he might smile, but then he bobbed his head once, turned and walked purposefully toward the trail without acknowledging the kids he met along the way. Elise followed, making certain to smile and greet those who continued to attempt to make Cody feel welcome. It was as if the children at Willow's Haven understood that, while they had each other for friendship and companionship and bonding through their situations, Cody had no one. Except Elise. And Jack.

Brodie and Savvy's home, a log cabin painted yellow, was situated a short distance behind the cabins for children and counselors, and Savvy exited her front porch as they passed.

"Not waiting until after breakfast?" She knew about their trips to Jack's place and had stayed up late last night discussing the guy with Elise. She, like Elise, didn't think he seemed dangerous, but she agreed that a man choosing to live on his own in the middle of the woods seemed odd. As did the fact that he didn't appear to do anything that generated any sort of income.

Cody stopped, glanced from Savvy to Elise, and still held that look of longing that she couldn't ignore.

"No, we're not waiting," Elise confirmed, while Cody appeared visibly relieved that the two women weren't going to require him to eat first.

A look of compassion crossed Savvy's features, and then she blinked a couple of times and nodded. "I understand." Elise had explained to the other woman the importance of getting Cody to spend time with the other kids, even if only during meals. Social interaction wasn't possible for someone who blocked himself off from the surrounding world.

An image of Jack flashed across Elise's mind. Jack, alone, by choice. Secluding himself from the outside world.

Savvy leaned over the porch rail as she spoke. "Cody, Dylan and the other junior high players have a football game tonight, and all of the kids here are planning to go. A bus is picking everyone up so that we can ride together. There will be popcorn and soda and cotton candy. I know he'd really like for you to watch him play."

Cody's eyebrows dipped, jaw tensed and mouth squeezed into that familiar flat line, but instead of acknowledging Savvy's request, he turned to face Elise head-on and lifted the hiking card.

The football game would be a great way to introduce him to the idea of joining the local school system while in a more comfortable setting than a classroom, so she wanted him to give it a try. But she also knew that getting him to go along with the idea wasn't happening without a little give-and-take on her part. "Cody, how about this—we'll go see Jack now—" she waited a beat for him to make eye contact and then continued "—and then later, after we've helped him with his furniture, we'll go to the game and support Dylan and his teammates."

He frowned, glanced toward the woods, then shrugged and nodded.

Elise smiled her gratitude to Savvy. "We'll be there."

Savvy blinked a couple more times, her eyes glistening with emotion. "That'll mean a lot to him, Cody. Thank you."

Again, the boy didn't acknowledge he'd heard, but he'd undoubtedly remained still for as long as he could manage, because he slapped the hiking card and then continued toward the woods.

Savvy waited until he was several feet away, then lowered her voice and said, "I think you're right… Whatever is happening with that Jack fellow is helping him. I asked Brodie if he knew anything about him, and he said he'd thought that cabin was still abandoned."

"Not anymore." Elise watched Cody and saw the flash card flitter from his hand a few feet shy of the trail. "I'll let you know if I learn any more about him today."

"I'll pray that y'all have a good day," Savvy said.

Elise thanked her and then left to catch up

with Cody. She'd take all the prayers she could get, not only for Cody, but also for her heart.

Her patient stooped to pick up the card from a pile of crushed leaves and dirt. She watched him gently wipe the bits of debris away and then study the image of the man. He seemed so intent on examining the hiker that he didn't notice Elise now stood beside him at the beginning of the trail.

"That reminds you of Jack, doesn't it?" she asked softly.

He didn't look up but nodded once.

Not wanting to stop the limited form of communication, she continued, "Does it remind you of your dad too?"

She expected another nod, but after a brief hesitation, he shook his head. He made no effort to start walking and remained transfixed on the image, so Elise suspected there might be an even more personal reason for his connection with Jack. "Cody, does that picture remind you of...you?"

He didn't nod, didn't acknowledge any response to her question. For a moment, she thought he'd changed his mind about seeing Jack, because he simply stood there staring at the card for over a minute while Elise silently asked God for any help He could provide.

Then a single teardrop fell onto the card.

Elise's heart clenched tightly in her chest.

Cody wiped the damp spot away with his thumb. His Adam's apple pulsed with a thick swallow, and then without making eye contact, he forged ahead.

They walked in silence, as usual, but Elise did her best to initiate any type of communication by admiring the natural beauty of the woods.

"I love the smell of the forest." She inhaled the earthy scents of damp leaves and crisp pine. Even though most flowers were no longer blooming, she still spied bits of deep scarlet and golden-yellow wildflowers against the dark brown base of the trees. The heady scent of the blooms added yet another layer to the blended fragrance of the woods. "Don't you, Cody?"

He never broke stride.

Undeterred, Elise continued, "There's a state park not far from my apartment in Birmingham. Oak Mountain State Park. Several of my coworkers hike there often, but I've never taken the time. Now I'm seeing what I missed."

Cody stopped, tilted his head toward a sound nearby. Elise heard it too, an animal rustling through the woods. She didn't think there were any bears in this area and suspected it was probably a deer, maybe a fox. She'd also seen a rabbit on one of her hikes and, of course, several squirrels, but this sounded larger than any of those. She appreciated the reminder that they were passing through God's incredible masterpiece and pondered whether the Garden of Eden had been similar to this. "Wow, it's peaceful out here, isn't it?"

"I've always thought so."

An instant waterfall of goose bumps raced down her arms with a vengeance. Elise whirled to see the owner of the deep voice that sounded scarily close. Close enough to touch her. Close enough to grab her. A yelp, or squeal, or something, escaped her throat as she turned, but her pulse thumped so fiercely she barely noticed. And then she recognized the intruder. "Jack! Are you trying to give me a heart attack?"

He retreated a step and held his palms toward Elise and Cody. "Hey now, I didn't mean to frighten you. I thought you heard me running." His broad chest moved steadily against a sweat-soaked T-shirt as he took the steady deep breaths that went along with a guy who'd been exercising.

"We," she managed, her own breath hitching as she spoke, "*didn't* hear you."

"Well, I sure heard you." His mouth edged up at the corners, and Elise would've taken a moment to appreciate how handsome he looked with that whisper of a smile if she wasn't still ticked that he'd scared her to death.

"You knew I didn't hear you," she said, at the same moment that Cody stepped beside her and reminded her that she wasn't the only one on the trail. He'd also been the first one to stop and tilt his head when *he'd* obviously realized the sound they heard was more than a small animal.

Elise needed to work on her survival skills.

"I'm sorry," Jack repeated, without the smile. "I really didn't mean to scare you."

She hated herself for wanting to see that semblance of a smile again. "No problem." Even as she uttered the words, she knew the statement wasn't true, because she did have a problem. A big one, probably six foot plus, if she had to guess. And standing very near.

He constituted a very substantial problem.

Because she now had another impression of the man who lived in the middle of the woods. She'd seen rough-and-wooly bearded Jack, and he'd captured her interest. Then she'd met clean-shaven-and-dreamy Jack, and he'd reminded her of how it felt to experience genuine attraction. But today, breathing heavy from his run, cheeks tinged red and hair damp from exertion, along with the casual exercise attire of a gray T-shirt with navy sweats...he suddenly hit approachable Jack. Desirable Jack.

She'd experienced this kind of head-spinning attraction only once, on the day she met Anthony, and she knew the appeal caused her to overlook the obvious, that this was the exact type of man she didn't need in her life. A guy with more than mere skeletons in his closet. A tormented past, a tortured soul and a broken man who, no doubt, she'd try to repair despite her vows otherwise.

"I'm sorry," Jack repeated. "Really, Elise."

The goose bumps made a reappearance when he said her name, and it had nothing to do with being scared.

"It's fine. No worries, okay?" She did her best to slow her racing heart and silently reminded herself of what happened the last time she let an instant attraction get the best of her.

Cody stepped between them and thankfully broke the moment. He pointed to the hiking man pictured on the flash card and then frowned at Jack.

"I…" Jack looked to Elise for a clue, but she remained silent. "I…went running," he finally said, "not hiking. I run in the mornings." When Cody didn't look pleased with his answer, Jack again looked to Elise, his confusion clearly visible on his features.

"He sees that guy on the card as you," she explained diplomatically and didn't add that he also saw the guy as himself. "But I think Cody is pointing out that you don't look like that today. You're—" she paused, swallowing as she took in Jack's running clothes "—dressed differently."

That was an understatement, and Elise did her best not to convey her opinion of the new look in her tone. Because her opinion was off the chart.

He looked at her for a brief moment and she thought she saw understanding dawn in his eyes, but then she saw the walls come up. He wasn't ready to let her get too close, which was good, because she didn't need to get too close to Jack. Ever. He was a means to helping Cody, and she'd do well to remember that.

Jack turned his attention back to Cody

before answering. "I wear workout clothes to run in the morning." When Cody's eyebrows dipped and he looked disappointed, Jack added, "But I'm on my way home now. I didn't expect y'all this early." He continued shifting his weight from foot to foot in a light jog as he talked, and Cody instinctively started a light jog too.

"We hadn't planned to come this early," Elise said, and then amended, "Or I hadn't, anyway."

Jack indicated Cody's feet. "You want to run with me the rest of the way?" Even as he asked the question, Elise noticed he looked a little uncertain about how he wanted Cody to answer. Had he been secretly hoping they wouldn't come today? Or ever again? After all, the guy had bought a cabin in the middle of nowhere; surely he hadn't planned on a kid like Cody, or anyone else, happening upon him in the woods.

But he'd said he wanted to help Cody.

And Elise believed him.

Why had she believed him? And why, even now, did she think he didn't mind them invading his private space again?

Cody looked from Elise to Jack and then stuffed the hiking flash card in his back jeans pocket. Then he nodded at Jack before increasing his jog in place.

For a brief moment, Jack didn't look so guarded. "All right, then, let's go." He jogged ahead, and Cody followed. Elise stood dumbfounded for a moment, until he yelled over his shoulder, "Come on, Elise!"

Another command delivered as though he owned the world, and she found her feet following the order, jogging behind the unlikely duo through the woods. An attractive, intriguing and undeniably broken man and a sweet, misplaced and equally broken boy.

Both running ahead of Elise.

Both running away from Elise.

Would she ever mend the boy? Or the man? Could she catch them, help them see the direction they *should* be going, instead of running aimlessly through the woods, aimlessly through life?

Or would she, like the times of the past, find herself feeling as lost and broken as the ones she chased?

Chapter Five

"The planer should be here soon, and then we can finish the dresser." Jack focused on Cody and did his best to keep his attention off Elise, jogging toward the cabin with wisps of hair escaping her ponytail.

His attempt was futile, because he couldn't take his eyes away.

She wore a light green T-shirt and jeans, nothing fancy or flashy, but she wasn't the type of female who needed a lot of attention-grabbing clothes or over-the-top makeup to capture interest. She had an intriguing look, very natural in her surroundings, but with those doe eyes, shiny dark hair and full lips, she claimed more than a hint of exotic appeal. But even more than her exterior beauty, the layers of depth and compassion that had her choosing a profession to help children like Cody and then following him through the woods each day because he wanted to work on furniture, of all things, with Jack… *that* was the kind of interior beauty that truly appealed.

As always, his thoughts moved to the big screen and a heroine like Elise who grabbed an audience by the heartstrings and made them root for her, cry for her, cheer for her.

They trust you to give them a God-focused film, something that will make them cry, laugh, cheer…and pray.

Roland's words haunted him, as did his threat that Jack would hear from the studio's attorney. Surely the studio exec understood why Jack couldn't promote the film, or any film. And Jack shouldn't contemplate what audiences would like, not anymore. In fact, as soon as *Finding Home* finished at the box office, he'd be done with the film industry completely, exactly what he wanted.

And the other thing he wanted? To live here, on his own, away from civilization and away from reminders of everything he'd lost. Reminders of how it felt to have children, like the boy who showed up at his cabin each morning. Or a beautiful woman by his side, like the one standing in front of him now.

So very different from Laney, yet Elise reminded him of why God created woman for man.

But God also took the woman he'd loved away.

Heart seizing in his chest, Jack suddenly noticed Cody's puzzled expression, and then a matching expression from Elise.

What had he missed while battling the pain of the past?

"Jack? Are you okay?" Elise pulled at the hem of her T-shirt and shot a worried look toward Cody. She'd said something to him, and he'd missed the conversation. Cody's mouth stretched into that familiar straight line, and he glanced toward the trail. Would he run away like he had those first two days, because Jack had been so absorbed in his own internal struggles that he missed a social cue?

"Yes, I'm okay," Jack gritted out, though he knew it wasn't true. "What did you ask?"

She chewed her lower lip and also glanced toward the wooded trail. Jack suspected she contemplated heading out and never coming back.

Part of him wanted to tell her to do just that.

Then Cody started tapping his fingers together at his chest, the way he did when worried or bothered, and Jack suddenly wondered how JJ would have reacted if he'd been in the same situation as this child.

A thick lump settled in his throat, and he swallowed through the emotion that had his left eye twitching. "It's okay," he said to the boy. "Everything's fine, Cody. I just didn't hear the question."

Elise again looked at the woods, and then at Cody. Jack knew she wanted to leave, but he also knew she cared about her patient enough to stay put. So did he. Therefore, he'd stop letting his mind wander to the past and pay attention to the present.

"What did you say, Elise?"

She pointed to Cody. "Not me. Cody is trying to tell you something, or ask you something."

Jack knew the boy hadn't uttered a word, but he turned to him and asked, "What is it, Cody?"

He stopped the frantic tapping of his fingers and placed both hands beneath the '69 Camaro that centered his shirt, and then he patted his stomach.

Elise shrugged. "He was eager to get here,

so we didn't eat breakfast. Again. And I think your biscuits and honey were a hit, more appealing to Cody than the banana pancakes they were serving at Willow's Haven."

"Better than banana pancakes? Now, that *is* a compliment." He was pleased to see Cody's smile and grateful he'd gone to Stockville last night for more groceries. Though if he continued to have daily company from these two, he'd need to make the trip into the town more often. "I'll put some biscuits in the oven and get coffee and milk."

Cody's brows lifted, and Jack added, "And honey. I'll get the honey too. Sound good?"

Naturally, he didn't answer, but he bobbed his head and moved toward the computer Jack had left on the porch table.

"I was watching a video earlier on how to use the planer to fix our wood. You can watch it while I get breakfast ready, if you want." Feeling awkward, he realized he didn't know what to do with guests. It wasn't as if he'd ever needed to do a lot of entertaining. Laney had been the one to coordinate food and activities when they had company. Plus, the majority of their friends had been the people he worked with at the studio, and Jack hadn't spoken to most of them since the funeral.

He started the video for Cody, who seemed as interested in the how-to project as Jack, leaning forward to view the master wood-worker and studying the piece of equipment that could reportedly correct even the most uneven surfaces. Hopefully it'd do the trick for the mahogany, because Jack needed to show the boy that the wood was still useful.

And that Cody was still useful.

"Do you want me to help you with break-fast?" Elise made her way up the steps to the porch and stood close enough for Jack to see a light sprinkle of freckles across the top of each cheek. Odd that someone with olive skin had the charming accent. Intriguing.

Jack didn't want to be intrigued.

He could actually let her prepare the break-fast while he showered and put on work clothes, but he'd been comfortable—way too comfortable—with seeing her in his kitchen yesterday. He'd actually gone to sleep last night thinking about the feelings that had caught him off guard standing side by side at the kitchen sink. "No, I'll put the biscuits in and get the coffee started, and then I'll change into some work clothes. You can watch the video with Cody."

"You didn't have the chairs or table out here yesterday, did you?"

Jack had turned to go inside but halted with her question. Truthfully, he hadn't planned to make the purchase when he went into Stockville last night for groceries, but then he'd noticed the craftsmanship on these pieces outside of a local store and knew he could use them, for now. "No," he admitted gruffly, "I bought them last night."

Her eyes softened, and then she cleared her throat and asked, "You got them for us?"

Cody paused the video and turned to hear Jack's answer.

He swallowed, the feeling of being exposed creeping to the surface, but he wouldn't lie to Cody, or Elise. "I suppose I did."

Cody's flat mouth inched up on one side, and if a dimple would've popped into place, it would've looked just like a JJ smile. Jack's heart lurched in his chest. He was getting too close, caring too much, and he wasn't sure how to stop.

"Thanks," Elise whispered, the single word resonating with emotion that Jack didn't want to acknowledge.

He nodded stiffly, entered the cabin and hoped that he could somehow control the ability of the two people on the porch to see right through him.

Elise took a seat beside Cody as he studied the video of the carpenter showing how to repair a piece of marred wood. He had smiled when Jack said he bought this furniture for their visits. Another smile, due to Jack. But Elise wasn't complaining. She'd smiled too. The handsome hermit had a heart, though she was fairly certain he was doing his best not to show it.

The porch furnishings weren't cheap, either. He'd undoubtedly spent time finding the rustic wooden pieces that blended perfectly with his cabin's appeal. And he'd purchased four chairs and two small tables, definitely more than he'd need if he didn't expect company.

Until this week, he'd probably never anticipated needing porch furnishings, because he'd planned to hide out in isolation. Then Cody invaded his private haven. And so had Elise.

There was no doubt in her mind that God had a hand in this. She'd thought several times about the fact that Jack declined to say grace for their breakfast yesterday. But she didn't get the impression that he didn't believe. She sensed more that he not only wanted to retreat from the world, but also from God.

Why?

A bell sounded as a notification came up on the computer.

Cody tugged at her sleeve and pointed at the text bubble on the screen.

Answer your phone, Simon.

Cody grumbled, then moved the cursor to collapse the bubble and resume watching the video.

But Elise stared at the spot where the image had been. Simon? Who was Simon?

Before she could wonder further, another bubble appeared.

Roland isn't blowing smoke. He's serious. And if you continue to refuse, the ten percenters are going to be pretty angry. That's a year's pay you're messing with, Simon. A lot of people are counting on you, including me.

Elise barely read the message before Cody, still grumbling, closed the bubble.

And like before, another one appeared. This time Elise noted the bold information at the top. No name, but a phone number with a 323 area code. Where was 323?

Answer your phone. Call Roland, or at least call me. Let me work this out for you. That's my job. Let me do my job, Jack. Please.

Jack. This time, the sender used his name. But why had he called him Simon? And who was Roland? What was a ten percenter?

Elise had so many questions, but should she ask? She shouldn't have read the text messages sent to Jack, but if he had the app on his computer, he'd eventually see the texts had come in, and he'd know that she had seen them. Wouldn't he?

So she should ask.

Or *should* she?

What, or who, was Jack hiding from?

What if she'd actually put her patient at risk by spending so much time with a guy who harbored dangerous secrets? Cody pointed at the screen, where a woman had joined the carpenter to help him guide the wood through the machine. In a few minutes, she and Cody would probably be helping Jack in that manner. The door opened, and the smell of coffee teased her nostrils as he exited with a steamy mug in one hand and a glass of milk in the other. He placed the glass on the table beside the computer for Cody and then held the mug toward Elise.

He glanced at the computer, and she wondered if he already knew that they had seen the texts. He probably got a notification on his phone too, right? But those sea-foam-green eyes didn't show any sign of suspicion but instead seemed guarded and cautious. He didn't look dangerous—he looked vulnerable. And Elise didn't have a desire to flee; she wanted to stay and put his fear at ease. She wanted to help him, the same way she'd wanted to help her father and the same way she'd wanted to help Anthony.

Elise begged her father to get treatment for the depression caused by his Asperger's. More specifically, for the depression caused when her mother left him *because* of his Asperger's. He'd declined, and he'd been a sad, lonely man until the day he died.

And Anthony. She'd tried everything to help him with the acute depression that he simply couldn't overcome. Medication. Psychotherapy. There wasn't anything she'd learned in her studies that she didn't suggest, and that they didn't try.

But it wasn't enough.

God, You know my weakness. Don't let me get hurt again. If it be Your will, take this desire to fix this man away.

"We can eat at the table out here today, if you want." His voice came out scratchy and raw, and she knew this show of hospitality to the two people who had invaded his privacy didn't come easy.

The desire to fix him didn't budge.

What are You doing to me here, Lord?

She took the coffee. "That would be great. I appreciate you getting the table for us, Jack."

Was he really Jack? Or was he Simon? And how would she ever know?

The day passed in a blur, with the planer getting delivered, and then the three of them working together in much the same way as the carpenter and his assistant worked together in the video. And, as Jack predicted, the machine corrected the imperfection in the now beautiful piece of wood.

Cody had smiled several times throughout the process and, at one point, Elise thought he had considered saying something, but then the moment passed. However, he seemed to be getting closer and closer to true communication again because of this man.

And Elise was growing more and more curious about who this man really was.

Her phone buzzed in her pocket, and she stopped sanding the side panel to view the text from Savvy.

We are about to start the devo. Are y'all coming?

Elise glanced at the time. She'd known that they had been working awhile but was surprised to see that it was already four in the afternoon.

Be there soon.

She sent the message and then watched Jack and Cody hauling wood for the next project that they'd selected, a wood plank dining table, around the side of the house. They worked together to lower the planks, but Cody dropped his too quickly, causing Jack's side to also plummet and smack directly across his feet.

Cody's eyes widened, mouth stretched into a hard straight line. He jerked his attention to

Elise and looked horrified that he might have injured his mentor.

But then Jack laughed, not a soft chuckle, but one of those yes-this-hurts-but-it's-funny laughs. "Don't worry," he said when his laughter subsided, "it stings, but you didn't take out any toes."

Elise watched as Cody's mouth slid into a smile, and then he released a little chuckle too.

A laugh. From *Cody*. Her throat pinched tight and her eyes blinked against beckoning tears.

Jack must have sensed her watching, because he glanced over his shoulder and looked directly at her. How could a man who could do so much for a boy who'd been through what Cody had experienced...be anything but good?

Answer your phone, Simon.

She recalled the odd texts. How could those have been intended for him? But the last text had actually called him by the name she knew—Jack.

What did it all mean?

Her phone buzzed again, and she pulled away from the intense connection with Jack to read the next text from Savvy.

Great. And we will leave for the football game as soon as the devotion ends. You can let Cody know that a friend of mine is planning to drive his antique Mustang to the game. I think it's a '66 maybe? He told me, but I don't remember the exact year. I know how Cody likes those old cars though, so maybe that will make him happy.

Elise looked up to see Jack still stared at her.

"Everything okay?" he asked casually.

Her skin tingled from the reminder of how it felt to hear a man ask her that simple question. Moreover, to hear *Jack* ask.

"Yes, everything is good. I just didn't realize how late it'd gotten." She directed her voice toward Cody, "That was Ms. Savvy. She said they're getting ready to start the afternoon devotion and are waiting for us."

He looked at the wood planks at his feet and frowned. Clearly, he didn't want to leave.

"She also reminded me that we will leave for the football game right after the devo."

His shoulders dropped, frown intensified to the point that his entire face sagged.

Then Elise remembered the rest of Savvy's news. "And she said that she thinks a friend of hers is driving an antique Mustang to the game tonight. If he does, I'm sure he'll let you look at it."

Cody's back straightened, eyes widened and mouth pushed into an instant goofy grin. Then he started toward the trail at a near run, jogging past Elise without looking behind to wave goodbye or even see if she planned to join him.

"Wow," Jack said. "He really does like old cars."

"He does," she said, wanting to follow after Cody but also needing to get some answers. "Just one second."

She texted Savvy to let her know that she'd be a little later getting back and received a response almost immediately that it wasn't a problem.

Elise was thankful for the new friend she'd found in Savvy and for the opportunity she had to talk privately with Jack. "Can I help you move that wood, since we won't be working on it until tomorrow?" She pointed to the stack he and Cody had dropped on the ground.

"I can get it." He lifted one shoulder in a half shrug. "I just asked him to help so he could, you know, feel useful. You can go on to the devo. You don't have to stay."

Elise sensed more to the statement than the fact that he didn't need help moving planks of wood. He didn't *want* help. Thought he could soldier on alone.

But her instinct told her that wasn't true. And she needed help too because in spite of her past experience, she couldn't stop that urge to find out what was wrong in Jack's world and fix it.

"Who is Simon?" she blurted, as her phone, still in her palm, rang loudly.

She saw the surprised look on his face at her question, but a glance at the display on her cell showed that the call was from Claremont Elementary, the school Cody would attend. She'd been waiting for this call. "I'm sorry. I have to take this."

She could almost see the relief on his face. Did he think she wouldn't want an answer to the question now? Or was he thankful that he had time to fabricate one instead of telling her the truth? Either way, she had to find out how long she had before she had to meet with the school about Cody. "Hello?"

"Hello," the woman said. "Is this Ms. Ramsey?"

"Yes, this is Elise Ramsey. How can I help you?" She knew why the lady was calling, and she was glad Cody had made some progress, but he hadn't made near enough for what this woman would want. She said a quick prayer that the inevitable meeting would be later rather than sooner.

"This is Mrs. Tucker at Claremont Elementary. I wanted to let you know that in accordance with the state's time restrictions, we have scheduled Cody Miller's IEP meeting for the second week in November. Of course, the state would like for you to be a part of this evaluation. Will Thursday, November 10, at one o'clock work for you?"

"That's only two weeks away." Elise needed Cody to communicate by the time that meeting took place, or he'd have to essentially start over in school, placing him in a special needs classroom instead of integrating him into the general population. "He had been mainstreamed last year, and I had hoped to have him ready for that again before he returned to the school system."

"We do have Cody's previous school records and those will definitely be taken into consideration. However, I'm sure you understand that we have to look at his current situation and establish our goals for him based on where he is now rather than where he was a year ago." She paused, exhaled heavily through the line. "I know his case is different than most children who are scheduled for an IEP, Miss Ramsey, but unfortunately, his unique circumstances are why we are doing this reevaluation." Another beat of silence echoed through the line. "So will that time and day work for you? We do value your opinions as part of Cody's IEP team."

"Yes, I will be there." There was no way she would miss advocating for her patient.

"We will see you on the tenth, then. Have a blessed day."

Elise disconnected and scowled at the phone. Have a blessed day? How was she supposed to do that after learning she had merely fourteen days to get Cody out of his shell and prove to the other members of his IEP team that he was ready to be mainstreamed?

Because Elise knew he was ready.

She'd seen him interact with Jack, even if nonverbally. And she'd witnessed his intelligence firsthand, in the way he read and followed the instructions for building the dresser, and in the way he handled himself in the library earlier this week. And, well, just by being Cody. He was smart and intuitive and sensitive...and he'd touched her heart deeply, maybe more than she'd even realized until this moment.

He was the closest thing to a son that she'd ever had.

She closed her eyes and bit back the urge to cry. She couldn't stand the thought of Cody digressing in school over something he couldn't control.

God, please, help me.

"What's wrong?" Jack's words were delivered softly near her left ear, and Elise was surprised to realize that he'd moved toward her and now stood close, very close, close enough that he eased his arms around her, enveloping her in a comforting warmth that she so desperately needed. She melted into the embrace, rested her head against his strong chest and found the courage to confide her fear.

"I'm afraid I won't have him ready in time." She couldn't manage more words than that without crying, and she didn't want to cry.

"Cody?" he asked. "You're afraid you won't have Cody ready?"

She nodded, her senses soothed by the feel of him against her and by the crisp masculine scent of the man who'd been captivating her for days without even trying. How long had it been since she'd been held by a man?

She knew exactly how long, since the day Anthony took his own life, two years, one week and three days ago.

Jack held her close for another moment, the steady beat of his heart providing a calming balm to her troubled soul. She felt him swallow, heard him clear his throat, and then ask gently, "Ready for what, Elise? *What* are you afraid he won't be ready for?"

She blinked a couple of times, gathering her composure. She'd had patients who hadn't progressed quickly in the past, but she'd never gotten this upset over the situation; quite the opposite, she usually saw it as a challenge. But Cody was different. He didn't have parents who would go to the IEP table ready to do battle for their child. He would have Elise, only Elise, and she didn't want to let him down. But she couldn't let herself get dependent on Jack to see her through this.

Regrettably, she eased out of his embrace. Yes, he was helping Cody, but there was still way too much she didn't know about the man to let him get too close. And he was so very similar to the one who had nearly destroyed her heart. However, he did care about Cody, and he was her best shot at getting the boy where he needed to be before that meeting in two weeks.

An unexpected chill ebbed through her, and she already missed the warmth of his embrace. She thought he might say something, explain why he'd felt the need to comfort her or apologize for crossing the boundary of mere acquaintances by holding her so tenderly. But Jack didn't say anything. He stood rigidly still, the only apparent movement his chest rising and falling steadily as he repeated his question. "*What* are you afraid he won't be ready for, Elise?"

She moistened her lips, gathered her thoughts and said, "His IEP meeting. I had hoped to have at least another month to prepare him, to get him to achieve the steps that he'd accomplished prior to the accident, so that he could move ahead instead of backward. Cody doesn't deserve to be punished for something he couldn't control." In her mind, this explained everything, but the confusion in those incredible eyes said she'd only muddied the water.

"IEP?"

Dismayed that she'd become so used to conversing with her colleagues that she went into autopilot for describing her patient in a clinical manner, she explained, "I'm sorry. IEP is the individualized education plan."

"An education plan designed specifically for Cody," he said, obviously trying to understand why she was worried.

"Yes," she said. "An IEP is created for each special needs child, taking into account the child's strengths and talents."

He nodded as she spoke, and she sensed he processed the information in much the same manner as a patient's parents would. And oddly, in Cody's case, she felt like she belonged on that side of the table too, as the one most concerned about how the child's progress would be evaluated. And the one ready to fight on his behalf.

"So someone else defines the individualized plan for Cody?" he asked, confirming that he wanted to understand the process.

"Not completely. The IEP team meets to bring individuals with different perspectives and expertise toward a patient's case to the table. The team pools their knowledge and formulates the individualized education program for the child."

Again, he soaked in every word, then asked, "And you'll be a part of this team? You'll help determine what Cody's goals will be with his education plan, right?"

"I will, but I can only advocate based on what he is doing at this moment."

He deduced what she didn't say. "And he's still well away from the point he'd achieved prior to losing his family."

She hated admitting the truth, but she nodded. "As he is now, in spite of the fact that I will recommend placing him in a nondisabled room for the majority of his time at school, I can't back up that recommendation with verified achievements."

"So Cody won't have the opportunity to be mainstreamed, unless *you* can prove he is capable of functioning well in that environment."

She nodded once again. "I'll be the only member on the IEP team who has worked with Cody firsthand." She visualized the individuals who were typically present at an IEP table. "Usually, the team members are composed of the child's parents…"

"Which, in Cody's case, isn't possible," he said quietly.

"Exactly. And then there will be at least one regular education teacher, one or more special education teachers, a board member from the school system, and a state social worker who will be responsible for interpreting the evaluation results and discuss what instruction may be necessary for the child to succeed."

"And you're afraid the group will determine that Cody isn't ready to be mainstreamed again, even with your recommendation that they place him in the environment he was used to before?"

She recalled the last few IEP meetings she'd attended. "In almost every IEP meeting, the parents fight fiercely for their child to receive what they believe to be the best education plan for their specific child. Cody won't have his parents there to do that."

They'd moved apart when Elise had separated from his embrace, but he took a step toward her now, placed his finger beneath her chin and gently tilted her face toward his. "But he'll have you."

She swallowed, so moved by this man's obvious feelings toward the boy she'd grown to care about so much. "I have two weeks, just two weeks, to show them that he's ready. They will want to meet with him, see his progress, and if he shuts down—" she fought the sting of that possibility "—if he can't display his ability to function on his own in the classroom without a specialized instructor, then he'll be placed in a class that isn't going to challenge him. He'll…" She paused, worked her way through the emotion. "I'm afraid he'll give up trying."

"And if he shuts down like that, his chances of being adopted will disappear."

"They won't keep me around once he is placed in the school system. He'll work with the instructors at Claremont Elementary, and I'll go back to Birmingham to work with other patients, and I—" her deepest fear hit her hard "—I'm afraid no one else will care enough to fight for him."

He cupped her chin. "I care. And I want to help. *We* can get him ready for that meeting."

She believed him. No, Cody wouldn't have parents in his corner to battle on his behalf, but he had Elise…and he had Jack.

Answer your phone, Simon.

Elise had been so taken aback by the phone call that she'd forgotten the worrying texts from earlier. But she remembered now. How could she trust Jack to help her get Cody ready, when she didn't even know who he was? She backed away from the touch of his hand against her chin, broke the intoxicating connection of being so very close to a man who stirred her heart. "Who is Simon?"

For a brief moment, the color left his face. Then his jaw flexed, and the compassion she'd witnessed was replaced by bone-deep regret.

What had he done? Who was he hiding from? And why had she let herself become so close so soon? Because the thought that he wasn't what he appeared was almost as terrifying as the possibility that she would fail her patient.

"Tell me, Jack. Someone sent you messages this morning, and they were on your computer. I know I shouldn't have read them, but they popped up when Cody was watching the video. There really wasn't any way *not* to see them." Swallowing hard, she held his gaze. "And the guy talked about someone named Roland and things that you were supposed to do, or should have done. And he called you Simon."

He closed his eyes, took a long, deep breath and then let it out. "I'm Simon, or that's what some people call me. It's my last name."

"Your last name," she repeated numbly. "Jack… Simon." The name scratched at a memory. She'd heard it before but couldn't recall where. Was it on the news? Had he committed some crime that would warrant taking refuge in the middle of nowhere?

Fear shimmied down her spine.

Her phone buzzed, and she was intensely grateful for whatever text she'd received. Probably Savvy telling her the devo had ended and it was time to leave for the game. She didn't pull her phone from her pocket, though. She didn't want to look away from him, just in case she was standing this close to someone who'd done something terrible. She needed to leave. Needed to run.

Why did you let me come here, God? Please. Protect me. Help me get away from him now.

"Elise."

She sensed the agonizing pain in the single word.

"You don't have any reason to be afraid of me," he said, his words delivered softly, deliberately, as though he honestly feared she would flee.

Oddly, her feet refused to move. Maybe because she did feel something when he touched her, when he looked at her, or when he stood this close, close enough that she could see something different in his eyes. Sadness?

"You shouldn't be afraid of me," he repeated. "If anything—" he swallowed thickly, and then the corners of his mouth tilted down "—I should be afraid of you."

Her skin prickled. Him, afraid of her? "What? Why?"

"The first time I saw you, you were in the woods. Crying. You were in pain, the kind of agony that I feel every day I breathe. I see you like that all the time, sometimes when I look at you, other times when I dream of you."

The phone in her pocket buzzed again.

"I'm not the only one with a past I can't forget," he said gruffly. "Don't let my problems keep me from helping Cody. I understand what he's going through, and I care about him. I want—I *need*—to help you get him ready for that meeting, Elise. Let me."

Another command. Delivered from a man who, though she hadn't realized it, had seen her at her very weakest moment. And a man who'd awakened feelings she'd sworn to extinguish forever.

"I have to go." She turned and started down the trail, her feet moving quicker with each step, until by the time she neared Willow's Haven, she'd reached a full run. Running from the man who'd caused a kaleidoscope of emotions to overturn her world. Running from the possibility of trusting someone who would break her spirit again. And running from the fact that she suspected she'd left a piece of her heart at the other end of that trail.

Chapter Six

Elise had been too emotionally spent and too discouraged to annotate Cody's daily progress last night. So when she woke at six to the sound of rain on the cabin's tin roof, she grabbed her computer, opened Cody's case file and updated his status.

Thirteen days. She had merely thirteen days to get Cody ready for a meeting that would affect his placement in school and, most likely, his ability to be adopted. How was she supposed to accomplish all of her goals for Cody in less than two weeks when she'd potentially lost all progress made so far in a single night?

After learning Savvy's friend hadn't brought the Mustang for fear of the upcoming thunderstorm, Cody hadn't acknowledged anyone at the game. He hadn't wanted the

popcorn, cotton candy or soda that had been
provided by the school for all of the Willow's
Haven children. And when the bus returned to
the children's home after the game, he hadn't
even looked at Elise when she told him she'd
see him in the morning. He'd simply kept his
head down until he reached his cabin, then
entered without looking back.

As a counselor, she no longer had a course
of action for Cody's case. Her instincts had
told her Jack would prove to be the best
means of drawing him out of his shell, but
after what happened yesterday with the odd
text messages, plus the fact that Jack admitted problems in his past—and knew that she
had secrets too—she doubted they'd ever venture down that trail again.

She had no idea that anyone had seen her
the day she'd been crying in the woods. However, Jack had, and at her lowest moment since
arriving at Willow's Haven. She'd awakened
with hope and excitement about her first week
working with Cody, but then she'd looked at
the date on her computer...the day Anthony
died. And memories slammed her with a vengeance.

Entering their house with her arms filled
with groceries. Smelling the lavender-scented

candle she'd bought him to help him relax when he had a particularly tough day. Calling out to him that she planned to attempt his favorite dish, eggplant parmesan, and then they could spend the night cuddling on the couch and watching movies.

They'd been talking about having children, and she'd been very excited about that possibility. He'd had so much hope, and Elise felt she'd given him that hope. Ever since she'd told him she also wanted to have children, he'd been on cloud nine.

Yet that candle burned.

She'd unpacked the groceries and recalled the potent smell of the garlic as she pulled it from the Whole Foods sack. It was strong, almost strong enough to cover the scent of the candle.

But not quite.

Realization that something must have troubled him caused her to stop unpacking the sacks and start toward his office. When she'd left for work, he'd said he would have a list of potential baby names when she returned; he'd wanted a family name from his ancestors and intended to peruse the genealogy while she was at her office. He'd hardly seemed disappointed at all about his company downsizing and letting him go from his accounting job. Besides, Elise made plenty of income for both of them, and they'd be fine while he looked for another job. And worked on creating a new life.

The scent of lavender grew stronger as she put her hand on the knob of his office. She couldn't remember any time when he'd closed the door before. She called out his name, turned the knob and entered.

Elise closed her eyes, hoping to stop the image before it invaded her world again, but she saw it anyway. Anthony, facedown on the floor, a gun beside his right hand, a note beside his left...and blood pooled across the hardwood.

Heart racing, she opened her eyes and focused on the log walls, the computer in her lap, anything to clear the horrible image from her mind. Anthony had been so troubled. And with all of her experience, she hadn't realized how much.

Jack had seen her on the day all those emotions came to a head. Jack, also troubled. Jack, voluntarily withdrawn from the world. And Jack, perhaps her best means of helping Cody.

How *could* she help Cody without him?

Elise did the only thing she could think to

do. She slid her eyes shut, bowed her head and prayed.

Dear God, I know that everything is in Your control, and I know You have a plan here, but I need courage. You know how much I care about Cody and his progress. You know how much I want him to find peace in the world again and have the potential to be adopted and loved and part of a true family once more. He's hurting, Lord. And I believe You brought me here to help heal his pain.

Show me what I need to do. Give me the knowledge of what he needs most and let me get him ready for that meeting at the school. Open the eyes and hearts of those individuals at the IEP meeting to see what an intelligent and incredible young man Cody is. Please don't let them hold him back, Lord. And please don't let him get discouraged. Let him know how much he is loved by You. And let him know how much he is loved by me.

Her mind drifted to yesterday afternoon, and those final words from Jack:

Don't let my problems keep me from helping Cody. I understand what he's going through, and I care about him. I want— I need—to help you get him ready for that meeting, Elise. Let me.

Elise shook her head. She was always very focused when she prayed, yet thoughts of Jack had invaded the middle of her prayer. What would God think of that? Or had He pushed that memory forward, letting her know what she needed to do?

She continued her prayer.

Lord, is that what I need? To truly trust him? To let Jack help me get Cody ready for that meeting? Because I know he's hiding from something, and I have no doubt You know what that something is. How can I trust him with Cody when I don't know the truth of his past?

Dampness trickled from her jaw down the column of her neck, and she realized that, at some point during her prayer, she'd started to cry. She wiped the tears away without opening her eyes and completed her plea.

God, I don't know what You're doing here, or what You want me to do, but if I need to trust Jack, show me how.

Then she added the part that would probably be the toughest for her to understand.

And, as in all things, Lord, let me remember that everything happens in Your time, but if it be Your will, let Your timing allow

Cody to meet my goals for him...in thirteen days. Amen.

Opening her eyes, she saw her laptop screen had gone black, and she ran her finger over the touch pad to bring it to life. Cody's case file filled the screen, with her status still highlighted. She saved the file and closed it, causing the search engine window to appear.

She stared at the blank field that centered the search engine. Yesterday, she'd returned to Willow's Haven with just enough time to climb on the bus to go to the game. And when the group returned home last night, she'd been so downhearted that she'd merely taken a shower and then climbed into bed.

But now, with a little time on her hands and the computer in her lap, her thoughts centered on the name that had been stirring her brain since she heard it yesterday afternoon.

Before she could change her mind, she quickly typed it in the empty field.

Jack Simon.

Positioning the cursor over the search button, she started to begin the exploration into Jack's past. But then the memory of his statement yesterday caused her to hesitate.

You shouldn't be afraid of me. If anything, I should be afraid of you.

Why would he be afraid of her? And why *shouldn't* she be afraid?

The cursor moved as she pulled her finger away and debated whether she really wanted to know what would come up on the screen. Should she wait to see if Jack divulged his secrets, instead of hunting on her own?

I'm not the only one with a past I can't forget.

What past couldn't he forget? And did she have the right to find out, if he didn't know anything about hers?

Then again, he hadn't asked.

In any case, Jack Simon was probably a common name and would return a mass of results. How would she know which one had taken residence in the wooded mountains of North Alabama?

She moved the cursor to the end of the text field and added the one additional fact that she knew about the man.

Jack Simon film industry.

Before she could change her mind, she clicked the search button.

As she suspected, a bounty of results filled the page, but all of the articles and images weren't about an abundance of men named Jack Simon. On the contrary, every story and each photo showcased one particular man. The one who lived at the end of the trail. The one who had been so kind to Cody. And the one who had touched Elise's heart.

No wonder his name had sounded familiar. Jack Simon. He was *the* Jack Simon. Why hadn't it clicked before? Director of the first two Christian full-length films to hit number one in box office sales. *Jacob's Dream* and *The Journey*, two brilliantly produced, beautifully themed and spiritually moving films that had undeniably soothed Elise's troubled soul during one of the toughest times in her life.

He was *Director* Jack Simon.

I worked in the film industry.

That was how he described his previous work? Talk about an understatement.

Why would a man with that kind of notoriety choose to live his life in seclusion?

After the first two links, Images of Jack Simon composed one section of the page. Elise scanned the square blocks of pictures.

The first photograph showed a professional head shot of Jack with his hair spiked and messy but with precision perfection. A light five o'clock shadow spotlighted that strong jawline and made him look even more rugged than the full beard he'd sported the first day they'd met.

He looked like a guy who could be in movies, but the posters behind him didn't showcase him as the star; they displayed the actors of *Jacob's Dream* and *The Journey*.

Jack Simon. How had she forgotten the name? Or what had happened to the famous director's family?

She scrolled through photo after photo, each one punching her stomach a little harder. Jack on his own as a young, aspiring producer. He'd worked on a few television films and then tried his hand at his true love, directing Christian movies for the big screen.

Beneath one of the photos, a quote from Jack read, "I want the world to see the difference God can make in a regular person's life. That's my goal. That's my dream. That's what I want to portray on-screen. If I've done that, I've done what He created me to do."

Elise studied the photograph. There was something different about Jack in the photo, beyond the fact that he was in his early twenties and that, based on the information on one of the links, he was now thirty-two. Something more than the spiked hair and the five o'clock shadow.

And then she had it.

His eyes were alight with happiness, with hope, with dreams for the future.

The eyes that had captured her attention since that first day were the same unique hue, but nowadays they were guarded, cautious and often filled with an aching sadness Elise didn't understand.

Until now.

She moved past the individual photographs to the family photos. Almost all were taken on a red carpet, but none of them looked like traditional red-carpet pictures, where those photographed appeared in a textbook pose, like something they'd perfected in a mirror before arriving. Quite the opposite, Jack and his family appeared as if they were simply having fun, and a camera caught the action.

In the first photo, a young boy, probably around eight years old, had dressed identically to his father and even had his hair spiked in the same perfectly messy style. A pair of little girls wore matching baby blue dresses, and they obviously wanted the photographer to notice their glittery red slippers, because one held her foot in front of her and the other pointed to her shoe.

And the wife. She had one hand on Jack's chest, and the other at her heart as she leaned her head back with an obvious bout of laughter.

"Oh, Jack," Elise whispered, "your family is so beautiful."

Then she moved to the next group photo, this one similar to the first, except the children were older. The boy grinned broadly, with deep dimples accenting his smile, and the girls were laughing, their arms wrapped around each other as they doubled over with giggles. She read the identifier above the image. Director Jack Simon and family: wife, Laney, twin daughters, AmyJo and Sadie, and son, Jack Junior (JJ).

"JJ." Elise had been so concerned when Jack called Cody by the wrong name. "Oh, Jack, I'm so sorry." The boy favored his father, with the same hair and exquisite green eyes, but he had his mother's wide smile and deep dimples.

Then Elise drew her attention to Jack's wife, Laney. She hadn't seen the woman's face fully in the other photo, since she'd had her head tilted back, but she viewed Laney clearly now…as she gazed adoringly at Jack. He returned the gesture, so that the two of them could have been the final scene of a movie. Specifically, a romantic film that provided a picture-perfect happy ending for a guy who had to be one of the most handsome men Elise had ever seen…and a woman who complemented her husband beautifully in a golden-yellow evening gown next to his dreamy black tux.

"Jack. Look at you. You were so in love, and so was she."

But then the very next photo showed the portion of the man's story that Elise remembered hearing in the news. "Oh, Jack…"

The aerial image showed a demolished plane tossed across a large field like a jigsaw puzzle with missing pieces. Elise remembered seeing the photo before. It bothered her then, because she felt sorry for the renowned Christian director who had done so much to depict his faith on the big screen. But now that she knew the man, she felt so much more, and her heart ached painfully for Jack.

"Why, God?" She wiped tears from her cheeks and moved her hand to her mouth as she read the caption. Director Jack Simon was already in LA for the premiere of *The Journey* when the plane carrying his wife, Laney, twin daughters, AmyJo and Sadie, and son, Jack Junior (JJ), crashed in an open field. There were no survivors.

Not wanting to see the next photos, probably Jack at the funeral, Elise scrolled past the line of images and scanned the titles of the remaining articles. The last link pointed to a blog post from yesterday, by one of the more popular Hollywood entertainment magazines, and the caption mentioned the delayed release of Jack Simon's most recent movie, *Finding Home.*

Elise clicked on the headline to read the full story.

Damascus Entertainment is billing *Finding Home* as Jack Simon's most extraordinary film to date. However, industry insiders are still holding their breath to see if the studio will delay its release once again, due to the withdrawal of director Jack Simon from all forms of promotion...and perhaps production. Some have said the renowned director didn't oversee the final scenes, but the studio has denied that rumor, saying the film is an authentic Jack Simon production from the first frame to the last.

Set to release last November, merely one year after the death of Simon's family on their way to the premiere of *The Journey*, *Finding Home*'s release was postponed over a year, with a current release date of this Christmas Day. As much as every Christian wants to see Jack Simon succeed—moreover, as much as every Christian moviegoer wants to see *Finding Home*—this blogger is uncertain whether the reported last film made by the man who so boldly proclaimed his faith on the big screen...will ever see the light of day.

The pieces of Jack's confusing conversations clicked into place, and Elise replayed the one that now made the most sense.

Don't let my problems keep me from helping Cody. I understand what he's going through, and I care about him. I want—I need—to help you get him ready for that meeting, Elise. Let me.

How could she say no? He *did* understand what Cody was going through. Both Jack and Cody had lost their entire families, and he truly *needed* to help Cody. But Elise now realized that Cody, even though he couldn't realize it now, needed to help Jack too.

She closed the laptop and made up her mind. Somehow, she had to get Cody back to Jack's place. That was the only way she'd help Cody get better.

And the only way she'd help Jack get better too.

Who else could bring God to the screen the way he had done…twice? And from what she read today, he could make an even bigger impact with the film set to release in a couple of months.

Christmas Day. It'd been one of her family's traditions growing up to go to the theater and see a movie at the end of the celebrations. Since she was the sole female of the four siblings, her brothers typically let her pick the film. They gave her a hard time when she'd selected a princess one when she was younger, but still, they went. And even now that they were all grown, they still asked their "little sis" what she wanted to see on Christmas. Which was why two years ago, merely months after Anthony's death, she'd selected *The Journey.*

And God had started healing her heart that night.

You meant for me to meet him here, didn't You, Lord? You meant for Cody to find Jack in the woods and give him a purpose for living? And Jack does need to help Cody, doesn't he? He needs to help Cody...to help himself. To heal his broken heart.

A whisper echoed through her mind, that Jack needed her too, but she shook the idea away. Surely God knew that she was merely the mediator here. He wouldn't have expected Elise to play any bigger role than that, not after what happened with Anthony. He'd allow her to help Cody and Jack, but He'd also allow her to protect her heart from the potential of falling for another broken man. Surely.

A knock sounded at her cabin door, and Elise glanced at the clock on her computer to see that she'd been reading about Jack for over an hour and hadn't made it to the dining cabin for breakfast. Was Cody at the door and upset because she'd missed their morning meet time? She hadn't even dressed yet.

Clamoring off the bed, she pulled her robe around her shoulders to cover her pajamas, slid her feet into her favorite slippers, then padded toward the front door, where the knock sounded again. "On my way!" She had to yell because of the rain, pattering steadily against the tin roof.

Opening the door, she saw that Savvy, not Cody, stood on the other side, her blond hair soaked and flat against her face in spite of the bright red umbrella that she'd already dropped by her feet.

Elise gasped at the stream of rain dousing the porch in spite of its covering, the wind pushing the water to the point that it appeared to be raining sideways. She opened the door wide. "Come on in and get out of that mess."

Even though droplets of water caused her to squint as she entered, Savvy laughed. "I can't remember the last time it poured this hard. A lot of good that umbrella did, huh?"

Elise shut the door behind her friend and smiled. "You look like you just got out of the shower."

"I guess I did." Savvy pushed her wet bangs away, then used the back of her hand to swipe the droplets from her forehead. "I tried calling when you weren't at the dining cabin, but you didn't answer."

"My phone was charging in the other room. I must not have heard it ringing over the rain."

"I can believe that. It's pretty intense on the

tin roof. I figured the sound probably caused you to sleep through your alarm."

"Nah, I've been up awhile. I've never been the type to sleep better when it rains, but I've known people who do." Anthony had claimed he got his best sleep when it rained. To keep Savvy from seeing what a toll that thought took on her emotions, she said, "I'll get you a towel," and darted toward the bathroom.

Savvy looked thoughtful as she returned to the room and gave her the towel to dry her face. "Elise, are you okay?"

She hadn't realized she was that transparent. And she didn't want to discuss her deceased husband with Savvy. Or anyone else. So she pasted on a smile. "Yes, and I'm sorry I missed breakfast. I was surfing the web and lost track of time."

"No problem. Happens to the best of us." Savvy gently pulled her fingers through her wet hair to remove the tangles, used the towel to dry some of the water away, then shivered. "Hey, you wouldn't happen to have some coffee ready, would you? That rain is pretty cold."

Elise shook her head. "Not yet, but I could use a cup, as long as Cody isn't waiting for me. I kind of expected to see him when I opened the door."

"He's not waiting," Savvy said. "That's partly why I'm here, to let you know that."

"Is something wrong with him? Is he sick?"

Savvy shook her head. "I don't think so. But he is refusing to leave the cabin. His cabin counselor let me know—that was why I was calling, to see if you wanted to try to persuade him to come out, or whether you wanted to give him a day off."

"Do you think he needs a day off?" Elise asked anxiously.

"I just know he was upset last night at the football field. And I felt terrible. I shouldn't have told you to tell him about the car. This is my fault."

Elise's throat pinched tight. She'd known he had digressed, as far as attempting to communicate in some manner, but she hadn't expected him to retreat from the world.

Like Jack.

"I'll get the coffee going."

Ten minutes later, she and Savvy sat on the couch sipping strong, hot coffee and discussing the problems both currently faced in life.

"So you're saying you have thirteen days to get Cody to communicate and interact with others the way he did when his family was alive?" Savvy took another sip of her coffee as she tried to understand the realm of an IEP meeting.

"Basically, yes." Elise also sipped her coffee, the warm liquid soothing her worries, but not nearly as much as having a friend to confide in.

It'd been a long time since she'd felt this kind of kinship with another female. When she'd been married to Anthony, he'd felt threatened by anyone who seemed to claim Elise's attention. She never discussed her work colleagues, because he assumed they meant more to her than he did. And she never went out with the other ladies at the office when they had their regular Tuesday night dinners, because that would leave him home, eating alone, and she'd been afraid of what his disposition would be afterward.

For a large portion of her marriage, she'd walked on eggshells. And she hadn't minded. She'd merely hoped and prayed that he would get better.

"So, since he's refusing to leave the cabin, what will you do? I mean, should I tell his counselor to try to make him leave?" Savvy frowned as she held the mug between her palms. "I don't even know how we would do that, since he's refusing to communicate, even with his flash cards. He did eat breakfast, but the counselor had to take his tray to the cabin."

"I don't think we should try to force him to leave." Elise indicated the ceiling, where she clearly heard the rain wreaking havoc against the tin. "It's not as if we'll be doing anything outdoors today. And while I suppose the dining hall is an option, if he wouldn't go there to eat, do you really think he'll want to be there for reading or schoolwork?"

"I see your point. But how are you going to get him to progress and be ready for that meeting if you don't get him to come out?" Savvy sipped her coffee and then added, "Mark, his counselor, did say that Cody had been reading every time he went to his room to check on him."

That sparked Elise's interest. "Did he happen to say what he had been reading?"

"Car books, the ones he brought with him from his home."

Car books. Not furniture books. Which meant he might have moved on from his infatuation with Jack and returned to his previous fascination. "I still think Jack can help him." Elise barely spoke the words and wasn't necessarily saying them to Savvy, but naturally the other woman heard and responded.

"I've tried to find out more about that guy, asked around town when we went to the square to shop, but no one even knew that anyone had moved into the cabin. Mitch Gillespie did say that he and some of the guys he'd hung around with in school used to stay there when they went hiking as teenagers. He said the place is huge. I didn't realize it was that large."

Elise nodded. "It's a two-story cabin, but he hasn't done a lot with it yet. Just minimal furnishings for now." She didn't add that Savvy need not try to get information about the stranger in the cabin, since Elise now knew everything she needed to know about who he was. And why he'd left his former life. She still felt a bit guilty about researching him online, but she was also glad she understood more about him and now knew that he was the perfect person to help her with Cody.

"Kind of odd that a guy would want a big cabin like that on his own." Savvy glanced upward as though trying to sort through the reasoning, and then she looked at Elise and said, "Maybe he's getting it ready for his family to move in?"

The photographs of Jack's family lingering on Elise's mind, she swallowed hard. "Or he could've just needed a place to be alone for a while."

Savvy nodded. "If that's the case, I guess he was surprised when you and Cody showed up."

"No doubt." Elise smiled over the top of her coffee mug and then sipped some more. She recalled her first impression of the rugged mountain man, when he'd had a thick beard covering that incredibly handsome face, and then every impression since. She'd discovered so many layers of the man in appearance, and this morning she'd also unearthed the depth of his suffering and reason for his retreating from society. And most likely, from God.

Both women jumped as a loud crack of thunder shook the cabin.

"Whoa, I think that must have hit a tree nearby." Savvy moved to the window and peeked through the blinds. "At least we've still got power. We've got one generator, but it'd only produce enough electricity for one cabin. Our cabins are plenty big enough with everyone divided, but if we all had to cram into one, it'd be pretty miserable."

"Willow's Haven is pretty packed now, isn't it?"

"Forty-eight kids and fourteen staff members and counselors, the maximum amount we can have." Savvy dropped the blinds back into place and turned around, pushing her damp hair behind her ears. "I got a call yesterday asking if we could take three brothers who were placed in the system due to neglect, and I had to tell them we were maxed out. I can't tell you how much that bothers me."

Elise had been with Savvy twice to visit churches nearby and discuss the need of adoptive families and foster parents to care for the children at Willow's Haven. If they could place the current children at Willow's Haven in homes, then they could help more children, which was Brodie and Savvy's goal. "What can we do, other than talking to the churches the way you're already doing?"

Savvy shivered, and Elise grabbed a brown-and-red afghan off the back of a rocking chair near the window and handed it to her. Savvy gave her a soft smile as she wrapped the afghan around her shoulders and returned to the couch. "As far as what else we can do, I did talk to one of the larger Christian children's homes in Atlanta yesterday to ask how they go about finding families for placement or adoption."

"What do they do?" Elise curled her feet beneath her on the couch. She prayed that the other place had an idea of what they could do to help the kids at Willow's Haven, like Cody, find a new "forever home."

"They use something visual. I hadn't really thought of it before, but when Brodie and I are talking to churches about needing families to follow Christ's example of loving others by loving the children in our home, we're only giving them words. We're *telling* them what they should feel, what they should do, but we aren't *showing* them. There's a big difference in how it affects the heart, don't you think? Whether you can actually *see* the ones affected by your actions."

"They need to see the children." Elise picked up their mugs. "You want another cup?"

"Sure." Savvy tightened the afghan around her shoulders. "And yes, that's it exactly. And I got to thinking about the children we've placed so far. All of the families who have chosen to either foster or adopt kids from Willow's Haven have belonged to the Claremont Community Church."

"The church that Willow's Haven children and staff members attend on Sundays and Wednesdays." Elise poured the coffee and then returned with the mugs.

"Right." Savvy accepted the cup and blew against the steamy liquid before taking a sip.

"So the people at churches where you've merely talked about the kids haven't come forward to sign up for fostering or adoption." Elise again thought of Cody. If Brodie and Savvy couldn't place nondisabled children, how would they place an autistic child?

"No, not a single family."

But Elise thought Savvy's presentation was amazing. She'd talked about her best friend, Willow, explained how she passed away, leaving three children, and how Savvy and Brodie adopted Dylan, Rose and Daisy. And she'd had photos of their family as well as pictures of children from Willow's Haven who'd been adopted with their new families. She'd also had photos of the children currently at Willow's Haven and needing placement. "But I remember the pictures you used with your speech at the churches. You did have something visual for them to see."

"I know. But the woman who runs the children's home in Atlanta said that people are touched more when they get to actually meet the children, hear them talk, laugh, play. See them interact."

Just hearing the word *interact* with reference to placement in a home stung. Cody wasn't interacting at all now. "So you need to take children with you when you travel to the other churches?"

"I would," Savvy replied, "but that isn't the best scenario. The kids here have already been removed from their homes or lost their families. They see their regular church as something of a home too, at least until they are placed. It isn't good for them to miss their classes at Claremont Community Church."

Elise drank a long sip of coffee. "So what does the Atlanta home do when they visit other churches?"

"Videos." Savvy lifted her eyebrows and bobbed her head as though this was the perfect solution. "They take videos of the children that need placement. She said it's important to show them in all aspects of life, playing together, going to school, eating, laughing, enjoying life. She said if they are sad, that should be portrayed, as well. The people that view the video need to know what these kids are feeling."

"A video lets them meet the child by seeing him or her on-screen."

"And videos pull at the heart, you know? They make you realize that this is a real person, a child who needs love. The children's home in Atlanta has a Thanksgiving appeal each year that is composed of an emotional video that displays the children at the home that have no families."

"Wow," Elise whispered, imagining sitting in church and viewing children who simply need a loving home, someone who cares. "That would strike a chord in me too."

"I know. And I think we should do it, have a video made that really showcases not only what we offer children at Willow's Haven for potential donors, but also what families can offer these kids who truly need a home."

Elise knew that could work, and that it might be a better way of finding Cody a home. "You're wanting to show a video at churches on Thanksgiving?"

"I would, but Thanksgiving is a month away. I don't think we'd have time to find anyone to film the kids and actually produce a decent video by then. And I really don't want it to be rushed and compromise quality. This will potentially be our best means of finding families for these kids, so it needs to be top-notch. And I don't even know of any professional videographers near Claremont."

Elise knew someone who could produce the absolute best video about the children. Maybe not by Thanksgiving, but definitely by Christmas. And he'd know how to portray Cody, as well. "It'd be important to show how special each child is, so families would understand how every kid needs love."

Savvy sighed. "You're worried about Cody being placed, aren't you?"

The fear that no one would ever step up to give him a chance scared Elise more than she wanted to admit. She nodded.

"But he was getting better, until last night, right?"

"He was," Elise admitted. "And I haven't given up. I just have to help him beyond the barriers he put up when he lost his parents."

"Do you think you'll be able to get Cody where he needs to be before that meeting at the school?"

"I don't know, but based on the past week, I'm certain I can't do it on my own."

"You're talking about Jack, right? The guy in the cabin who's been helping with Cody?"

"Yeah. I may stimulate Cody's progress,

but I haven't achieved satisfying results on my own. Every bit of forward progress he's made has occurred because of his interactions with Jack."

"Do you think you'll be able to get them together again, now that Cody's shut down?"

Elise thought about that IEP meeting. The team would want to meet Cody, talk to him and see how well he could interact with them in order to determine how well he'd function in a mainstream classroom. "I have to."

"How are you planning to do that?" Savvy asked loudly, due to the rain increasing and beating a strong staccato rhythm that made her cringe.

"Honestly, I'm not sure. But I know I need to talk to him and figure out a plan of action." Elise flinched too, the rain coming down so fiercely that it sounded as though the roof might cave in from the attack.

"Talk to Cody?" Savvy finished off her coffee and placed the mug on the table.

"No, to Jack." Elise swallowed the last sip from her cup and nodded matter-of-factly to her friend. Her mind was made up. She needed to talk to Jack about Cody, and she didn't want to talk on the phone. She wanted to see him in person. And she wasn't going to analyze the reasoning for that.

She was just glad she'd packed a raincoat for this trip.

During the past two years, while he took the time to sell his home in LA, tie up loose ends and mourn everything he'd lost, Jack hadn't felt lonely. He'd been grief-stricken. Depressed. Disillusioned. Solemn. Despondent. A whirlwind of emotions that collided and cascaded over his very being each and every day.

But he hadn't felt lonely.

Until today.

With the appearance of Elise and Cody at his home over the past week, he'd experienced a hint of what a family felt like again, and now that he'd been reminded…he ached for it.

Yearned for it.

But he knew that would only cause heartache when he started loving a family like he'd loved his before…and then lost everything. He didn't want another woman in his world, didn't want other children. So it was probably a good thing that he'd never see Elise again, let alone Cody.

She was scared of him; he'd seen it in her

eyes. Scared because she had no idea who or what he was. But Jack had told her the truth. Elise had no reason to be afraid of him, yet he had *every* reason to be afraid of her. He'd come to this place to get away from the potential of being hurt again because he cared too much. If he wasn't close to anyone, then how could he be bothered when he lost them? Why would he care?

But now, because of Elise and Cody, he did care. About both of them. And today, when they hadn't shown up at their typical time, he'd assumed, probably correctly, that they'd never return.

He should be glad for that.

He *should*.

But he wasn't. And with every sound of thunder or rain, he wondered how they were faring at the children's home. Once he'd learned where the place was located, he'd purposely planned his runs away from the area. He didn't want to meet more kids at the home, because they might, like Cody, remind him of his children.

Jack also wondered if the reason they hadn't appeared this morning had more to do with the thunderstorm than the fact that Elise had clearly been freaked out about him when she left yesterday. Maybe she had planned to come and tell him that she realized how ridiculous that notion was, and that she and Cody wanted to continue spending time with him.

Or maybe the rain had nothing to do with it, and they wouldn't have come even if it were a clear day in June, because Elise had determined the risk wasn't worth the reward, if she had to bring Cody near a guy like Jack.

He pressed the button on the hot chocolate maker and watched the light brown liquid swirl as it heated. Might as well get some use out of the thing himself, since he wouldn't need it for company.

His phone dinged, which it'd been doing fairly regularly over the past couple of days, and he lifted it to view the text.

Roland has called in all execs today for a meeting about *Finding Home*. I suspect they're preparing to file suit for breach of contract. Is there anything you want me to say or do on your behalf?

Jack closed his eyes, counted to ten. He'd been ignoring Vincent's texts for days, but he wasn't in the mood to receive more of them today. He'd put a stop to it with a single word.

No.

Then he set his phone to vibrate and slid it to the back of the kitchen counter. There wasn't anyone he wanted to talk to. And even with that thought, he visualized Elise, stomping away through the woods in an effort to leave him as quickly and thoroughly as possible.

If he were being honest, there *was* someone he wanted to talk to. Elise Ramsey. The one person in the world who had the power to destroy him, to grab his heart, make him care…and then what? She'd leave? She'd said she would return to Birmingham after Cody entered the school system, which would be a few weeks from now. Jack would be stupid to have feelings for another woman who would be taken out of his life, even if not by death.

So why should he bother?

Because you want to help Cody, his mind whispered, and then, a faint addition, *and because you care about Elise.*

The truth of that infuriated him. He couldn't care for her, or anyone else, because he couldn't handle going through the loss if anything happened to her. He wouldn't.

And yet he wondered if she and Cody were okay in the storm.

Footsteps outside, on his front porch, caused him to leave the kitchen and start toward the door. And as he reached it, a quick rapping knock beckoned from his visitor.

God, he started, then scowled. Had he actually begun a prayer to ask Him to let this be Elise and Cody? He shook his head, grabbed the knob and opened the door.

Elise wore a light turquoise raincoat with a hood that framed her face and drew even more attention to her dark eyes, high cheekbones, full lips.

Had it only been a day since she'd left him standing in the woods? The truth of that question slammed his chest.

He'd missed her.

"I—" he started, then realized she'd come alone, "Where's Cody?"

A flicker of disappointment washed over her face, and though she masked it quickly, Jack hadn't missed the emotion.

"Is something wrong with Cody?" he asked, his voice gruff with concern.

"In a way." The skies were dark, in spite of the fact that it was just past noon, but a brilliant burst of lightning illuminated the sky and spotlighted the woman at his doorstep.

She was even prettier now, with the rain providing a veil between her and the wooded surroundings. And she looked at him…as though she'd missed him too.

Had she?

Elise glanced down, away from his penetrating stare, and Jack silently reprimanded himself. Yes, he'd missed her being here, but he didn't like the fact, and he wasn't about to tell her. He'd simply grown accustomed to company, and that desire would dissipate once Cody started at the school and then found a new home, and once Elise returned to Birmingham.

Then things would be the way Jack wanted.

"Jack, it's wet and a little cold out here. And I need to talk to you about Cody…" She shifted her weight from one foot to the other, and Jack noticed the turquoise galoshes that matched the raincoat.

It'd help if she were merely beautiful; she didn't have to be cute too.

"So can I come in?" she concluded.

He had lost his ability to think, because it hadn't occurred to him to do anything but gawk. He mentally slapped himself. "Yes, sure. Come on in." He edged back to let her enter, then watched as she slid off one of her galoshes and then the other.

Fuzzy pink polka-dot socks. *That* was what she wore beneath her rain boots.

She noticed where his attention had landed and wiggled her toes. "A gift from my oldest brother, Aaron. He knows I like warm socks, but he also likes to make them fun."

"How many brothers do you have?" he heard himself ask and then wished he'd stop trying to learn more about her. He needed to keep this relationship strictly professional. Even so, he awaited her answer.

"Three, all older. And all of them try to tell me what to do," she added, sounding like any younger sibling. He recalled AmyJo and Sadie fussing anytime JJ attempted to play boss.

"Big brothers are like that," he said, fondly remembering his son.

"Yeah, I've wondered how Cody was around his little sister and brother. I think he'd have been really helpful from what I've learned about his past."

Jack thought of how the boy had enjoyed sanding the furniture, putting it together and even hauling wood from the garage to the front yard. He hadn't complained; on the contrary, he'd smiled more than Jack had seen him smile at any other time. "I bet he was a great big brother," he said, noting yet another similarity to JJ.

JJ had been amazing with AmyJo and Sadie.

Cody deserved to be a big brother again, to have a family again.

As though knowing where his thoughts had headed, Elise said, "The Mustang he wanted to see wasn't at the football game last night. And he didn't take it very well."

"Is that why he isn't with you?"

"That, and I'm not sure he would have wanted to weather the storm, either. It's pretty rough out there." As though her point needed emphasis, a resounding boom of thunder caused her to jump. "See?"

"I do." He had thought about that all morning, whether the rain would keep them away. "I'm a little surprised you came out in this weather."

She shrugged. "I have thirteen days to make progress with Cody, and he's come out of his shell the most when he's with you. I wanted to discuss some ideas about how to help him continue to make progress." A heavy sigh escaped her, and she added, "And at the very least, get to where he was before that game last night. He was so disappointed, Jack. When we got back, he refused to even look at me when he went to his cabin, and this morning, his mood did not improve."

Jack hated that Cody had been so upset about the car. He'd seen how excited the kid got yesterday when he'd thought he'd get to see an actual vintage automobile at that football game. He couldn't imagine how crushed he'd been when he arrived at the field to learn there wasn't a vehicle to view.

A flicker of an idea played with his thoughts, about a boy who had one goal in life, something that seemed trivial to everyone else but meant the world to the kid. Yet he was locked within himself and couldn't explain the disillusionment of finding his hopes and dreams shattered.

It'd make a decent theme, something akin to the story of the Pharisee and the cup in Matthew.

"Jack?" Elise's eyebrows were lifted, mouth quirked to the side as though concerned about where his thoughts had headed.

So was Jack.

And then it occurred to him, she'd entered his house without stopping to question the safety of the action. She no longer had the fear that he'd seen in her eyes yesterday. "What happened?"

She looked even more confused. "What happened? To Cody? I just told you…"

"No, what happened to you? Yesterday, you were angry, and you were afraid of me. I didn't misread that. But today—" he shook his head "—that isn't the case. What's changed?"

She chewed her lower lip, glanced toward the kitchen. "Do I smell hot chocolate?"

Jack knew she evaded the question for a reason, but he also knew he was playing with fire, trying to figure the woman out. He needed to keep their conversations centered around Cody, not around the way Elise affected him when she was near.

Or when she wasn't.

"Yeah, I made some in case."

"In case what?" she asked, smiling as though she suspected the answer.

He wasn't going to walk into the trap. Not completely. "In case Cody came back. I thought he might like a cup of hot chocolate."

She looked skeptical but didn't comment. She merely walked toward the kitchen to look at the small white Cocomotion he'd purchased in Stockville. "This wasn't here the last time I was in the kitchen."

"No, it wasn't." He moved toward the cabinet to withdraw two mugs. "Do you want a cup? I—" he paused, felt a little foolish for the impromptu purchase "—I bought some of those small marshmallows and whipped cream if you like that."

Her mouth curved upward, and Jack was taken aback by the beauty of the subtle smile. "When did you buy the hot chocolate maker?"

Busted. "Last night." He poured the two mugs of chocolate. "So would you like the marshmallows, or whipped cream?"

"Whipped cream, please." She leaned against the counter, crossed her arms and watched him retrieve the red-and-white can from the refrigerator. "You bought that for me and Cody, didn't you?"

He refused to look at her as he topped her cup with the white foam. "I thought we might be celebrating Cody seeing that Mustang."

"So you bought a hot chocolate maker, cocoa, whipped cream and marshmallows."

"I wasn't sure what y'all would like," he said gruffly. Then, grabbing a handful of the marshmallows and tossing them in his cup, he turned toward the woman still staring at him as though she knew him inside and out. "Here you go."

She took the mug but never broke eye contact. And Jack was having a tough time looking away.

Finally, he shifted toward the counter, snatched his cup and said, "We can drink this at the table while we talk about Cody."

Cody. The only thing they needed to talk about. Not the way she looked cute in her fuzzy socks as she padded toward the table, or the way her oversize sweatshirt hung past her slender hips and made her seem even more petite. Like someone he should take care of.

"So have you had any ideas about how to help Cody now that he's retreated into himself again? That's why you came here on your own, right? To get a game plan together before that meeting—the IEP—at the school?" He took a sip of the rich chocolate and focused on how perfect the machine made the liquid, frothy, like the kind he remembered getting at ball games as a kid. JJ had loved hot chocolate. So had AmyJo and Sadie. He wondered if Cody did too.

"Is it okay if I'm completely honest with you?" she asked softly.

No. Jack wasn't certain whether he could

handle complete honesty. He took another sip of the chocolate and prepared himself for what this woman, who'd caused him to think and feel things he'd sworn he'd tamped down forever, would say. "Sure."

She tried to sip the chocolate, then laughed when the whipped cream hit her nose. She wiped it away with her finger, grabbed a napkin from the middle of the table and giggled. "I don't think I even got to the hot chocolate for all of the whipped cream."

Jack felt his face move into a smile. He couldn't help it. This was so very...nice. "I may have overdone it with the whipped cream."

"It's okay. I'll stir it up a little." Then she put her index finger in the cup and swirled it through the white cream to mix it with the hot liquid.

"I do have spoons," he said and couldn't hold back the grin that remained firmly in place. She seemed so at home here, in the middle of his cabin and sitting at his table. Not at all like the skittish woman who'd left in a rush yesterday.

"Oh, yeah, well, I've already taken care of it now." She did a little shoulder lift, put her finger in her mouth to remove the liquid and then took a big sip. "This is amazing. I've got to get me one of those machines."

Her contentment was palpable, but Jack was no longer content. He couldn't stop wondering what had changed. Why was she so comfortable around him now, after being so fearful only twenty-four hours ago?

"You asked if you could be completely honest with me." His smile had subsided. Something had happened, and he wasn't sure he wanted to know what. "Honest about what?"

"About Cody. The truth is—" she huffed out a little breath, blew on her chocolate and then took another sip "—the most prominent progress I've made with him is when he's with you. I honestly don't think I can get him ready for the IEP without your help."

Jack's chest warmed at the mere mention that he'd helped the boy. It wasn't what he'd expected her to say; nevertheless, it ignited something within him that he hadn't felt in a while. He'd needed to reach out to that kid even more then he'd realized.

Truthfully, he still did. He hadn't wanted to give himself the opportunity to open his heart to another child, or another woman, after losing his family. But he could almost feel the tight strings on his heart loosening, and he didn't know how to stop them from unraveling completely.

"So how can I help get him ready for the school meeting?" He sipped the chocolate, got a couple of the marshmallows in the swallow.

"That's the thing... I'm not exactly sure. I know that he has come more and more out of his shell and moved toward genuine communication, the kind he had before he lost his family, when he spends time with you."

"Well, that's easy, because I like spending time with him." He knew his next suggestion would only hurt him, only remind him more of what he'd lost, but there was no way he could turn his back on what Cody needed. No way he could turn his back on Elise, either. "You just need to bring him here each day."

Elise took another sip of her chocolate and seemed to ponder his recommendation before speaking. "That may prove to be a problem. He wouldn't come out of his room today, not that we have the best weather for hiking. But I don't know how long this disappointment about the car is going to affect him, and I'm genuinely afraid that when he does let me in again, I might be starting over at square one. And I don't have time for that."

Jack had been nurturing an idea, something

that he suspected might help Cody, based on what he'd learned about the boy. And he'd made a phone call earlier that would put that plan into play. "I have something for him to see. It'll get here on Monday. Do you think if you told him I had a surprise for him that he would change his mind about venturing into the world again?"

She bit her lower lip, looking as though she were trying to select the right words, and then sipped her cocoa. "I'm thinking that if anyone would know—" she took another sip "—what it would take to get someone who had retreated from the world to venture out again, it would be you." She paused, while Jack waited, unsure of what to say. "What *would* it take, Jack?"

He knew she no longer referenced Cody, but he wouldn't fall into that trap. They needed to discuss the child, not Jack. He didn't need help. "I've bought something that I want him to see."

Her head moved up and down in a conceding nod. "Okay. I'll leave it at that. You aren't going to tell me what you bought?"

He shook his head. In truth, he was as excited to show Elise as Cody, but he wasn't about to admit it.

She drank more chocolate, and this time, the foamy whipped cream lined her upper lip. But she didn't seem to notice.

Jack found himself staring at the white substance and wondering…things he shouldn't be wondering.

Her eyes found his, and she realized the problem, because she whisked the tip of her tongue across her lip to wipe the sweetness away.

Jack suspected her mouth would still taste like whipped cream.

Not that he would ever know. Or even wanted to.

The lie, even though merely thought to himself, taunted him.

He did want to know.

Jack attempted to push the unbidden feelings away, but he sensed the truth; those strings around his heart continued disintegrating. What good was a cabin in the middle of nowhere when a boy like Cody—and a woman like Elise—were at the other end of the trail?

"If you have a surprise for him coming on Monday, I guess I'll have to tell him that beforehand, and then hope that he'll be ready to start working with us again Monday morning.

But we'll only have ten days left. Do you think whatever you've bought is going to make that much progress that quickly?"

Thunder boomed in the distance, and the rain increased on the roof of the cabin. Even the weather knew what was happening with his heart. He knew there was nothing he could do to stop himself from caring so much; he simply had to help Elise get Cody ready so he'd have a chance at a family and so she would return to her home. *Then* he'd protect whatever happened to be left of his heart.

He cleared his throat. "We probably wouldn't get a whole lot done anyway before Monday. From what I read online, this thunderstorm is expected to last all weekend. And this surprise will be worth the wait." He drank more of his chocolate, ate a few more marshmallows and corralled his thoughts to the place where they should be, on Cody, instead of on Elise's mouth. And memories of how amazing it felt to hold a woman whom he cared about.

He needed to encourage her to leave. Now.

"You should get going before it gets dark."

Her brow lifted, luminous eyes looking up at him as though she knew where his thoughts had headed.

Did she know how much she affected him?

Did she realize that, merely by spending time with him and letting him see how much she cared for Cody and how thoughtful she was and how fun…that she'd reminded him of what he'd lost? And what he'd never have again?

"I think it's already dark," she said ruefully, "thanks to the storm."

Jack glanced at the clock. Only four in the afternoon. But a look out the window verified that it was even darker, even grayer, than when she'd arrived. "That's some storm."

"It is," she agreed, "but I don't think it's going to do anything but get worse. You're probably right… I should start back to Willow's Haven." She picked up her mug, then reached for his. "You finished?"

"Yes," he rasped, too caught off guard by having her offer to clean up at his house—and by how it felt to have her offer—to protest.

She took the mugs to the sink, rinsed them out and then padded past the table toward the front door. He watched her shove one fuzzy pink foot and then the other into the turquoise rain boots. Then she stood and put on her rain jacket, with one jeans leg bunched above one boot and the other extending to the ankle.

There was something very beautiful about marred perfection.

She turned toward Jack, looked as though she were going to say something, but again, changed her mind. "I'll do my best to bring Cody on Monday." She reached for the door, opened it, and a flash of lightning illuminated the streaming rain. "Whoa."

"Maybe you should stay here for a while." The minute the words were out of his mouth, he regretted them. And from the shocked look on her face, she knew it.

"Like you said—" she tugged the hood of her jacket over her head "—the storm isn't stopping. I should get back before it gets worse."

"Wait."

She paused, one hand on the door. "You're really accustomed to giving orders, aren't you?" She bit her lip, as though that very question had been what she'd fought not to say.

Jack *was* used to giving orders, but he always did it with respect and love. "I'm...sorry. But I can't let you walk back in that storm alone. I'll drive you back."

She glanced toward the storm, then toward Jack, and he saw the indecision pass over her face before she answered, "I wore my raincoat and rain boots. And it isn't that far of a walk." She bobbed her head as though cementing this conclusion in her mind. "I'm fine to walk. And it'll give me a chance to think about everything with Cody."

What kind of man would let her go out into the storm, walking through the woods, no less, alone? Not Jack Simon. If she wasn't going to waver in her stance to walk, then she wouldn't do it on her own. "Let me grab my coat and an umbrella. I'll go with you."

A worried look passed over her face, but then she gave him a subtle nod. "Okay."

Jack retrieved his coat and umbrella from the closet. He grabbed a flashlight too, for good measure, and said, "Okay, let's go."

Elise hadn't agreed to Jack's offer to drive her to Willow's Haven because she hadn't wanted to be alone with him in the confines of his car for the short duration of the trip. It'd seemed too intimate, too close, for her to get a grip on the turmoil of emotions that had pulsed through her ever since she learned about his past. She had every reason to ward off another attraction to a man with more than his share of pain, more than his share of heartache. She needed to keep their relationship focused on Cody.

Riding in a car with him had screamed bad idea. Bizarrely, walking beside him through the woods in the middle of a rainstorm... seemed even more of one. She hadn't gained the courage to tell him what she'd learned this morning, yet she couldn't help but feel closer to the man simply from knowing his story.

They walked in silence, but because they shared the umbrella, they walked closely. Very closely. So close that he had one arm wrapped around her to guide her steps, and so close that she could catch the scent of his aftershave every now and then. The flashlight illuminated the rain tumbling sporadically through the trees, some places merely sprinkling, and others pouring with a vengeance...causing Jack to pull her closer.

She was surprised that, regardless of her attempt to make this journey alone, she was glad he'd insisted on accompanying her. Because in spite of how scared she'd been of him yesterday afternoon, after learning the truth, she felt undeniably safe. Secure. As though nothing could harm her as long as she remained under this umbrella with Jack.

He nodded toward the last fork in the trail

leading toward Willow's Haven. "That way, right?"

"Yes." She let him guide her down the path until she saw the lights from the circle of cabins for the kids. The dining cabin, at least double the size of the remaining ones, shone brightly at the far center of the property, though the golden light from the windows looked blurry through the rain. "That's it," she said, stopping on the trail. "I can make it the rest of the way with the raincoat."

"Are you sure?"

His concern touched her, especially now that she knew his heart. He wasn't anyone to fear, quite the opposite. This was a good man, a man of faith, a man who'd suffered unspeakable pain.

She longed to help him heal. And she feared how that longing might affect her heart.

"Yes. I'll be fine." She had pushed her hood down while they were beneath the umbrella, but she reached for it now. It had bunched in the back or was caught on her hair, because in spite of her tugging, it wouldn't move.

"Here, let me help." Holding the umbrella and flashlight in one hand, he used the other to gently slide the hood over her head.

Elise stood very close to him; she had to,

to stay out of the rain. So when she glanced up, the golden hue from the flashlight highlighted his features so that she could see the way he looked at her. She saw the questions in his eyes—and how he was torn inside. He'd wanted to hide, wanted to be alone and away from every aspect of a world that had hurt him so deeply. Yet here he was, walking with her, protecting her from the storm.

She didn't let her own fears hold her back. She had to let him know how much she cared and how very much she wanted him to heal. She lifted her hand and touched his face, ran her fingertips along that strong jaw and watched the play of emotions when he realized what she was doing, and what she wanted.

"Elise." His head shook subtly, but as she slid her hand to the back of his neck and eased his face closer to her own, he didn't stop her.

She hadn't experienced the power of a kiss in two long years. Hadn't wanted to be that close to anyone again. But she wanted this, and as their lips met, she melted against the man whose world had been shattered yet who had nevertheless touched her heart in immeasurable ways.

She felt him respond to the kiss, knew he

was as swept up in the moment as she was, and then…

Jack pulled away, his eyes filled with torment. "Elise, that…that isn't what I want. I can't. It's…" He took a deep breath, closed his eyes and let it out slowly. "It's too difficult for me, and it always will be. That's why I'm here. There's no way you can understand…"

She couldn't let him continue. "Jack, I know. I know who you are. I know—what happened to your family." She wanted to wrap her arms around him and hold him close, but he moved even farther away, so that she was certain the falling rain soaked his back.

More anguish filled his eyes. "You…know? How long?" The two words were short and clipped. "How long have you known, Elise?"

"Since this morning. Jack, it's terrible what happened, and I know you feel like you can't continue living the way you did before, but God has given you so much talent, and He can help you, and so can…"

"He can *help*?" His jaw clenched, mouth rolled in as though he had to physically cut off the next words he'd wanted to say. He jerked his head toward the cabins in the distance. "You've got this, right? You don't need me anymore."

Elise swallowed. Nodded. "I'm sorry, Jack."

"Goodbye, Elise."

She had nothing left to say, so she turned and walked away. Her feet slapped through puddles as she progressed toward the cabins without looking back. Had he watched to see if she made it safely, or had he turned away completely?

It didn't matter. She shouldn't care. She'd done it again. Tried to help a man who couldn't be helped.

Thunder boomed. Lightning cracked. Her heart clenched.

What had she done?

She prayed that Jack would forgive her. And she prayed the rain disguised her tears.

Chapter Seven

Jack kept himself busy all weekend, in spite of the ceaseless rain, to keep his mind off that last conversation with Elise.

And that kiss.

She'd stirred emotions inside him that he didn't want stirred. Started him thinking about things he didn't want to think about. He'd moved here to keep from wanting everything he lost, and Elise—and even Cody—were blatant reminders of the pain.

And he was angry with her, felt betrayed by her. She knew the truth of his past. She'd mentioned his talent and what happened to his family. And then, as if that weren't enough, she'd added that she believed God could help.

God had done enough.

But despite how furious he'd been on Friday, as he prepared for the finishing touches on the dresser, he found his attention continually veering toward that opening in the trees, to the place where Cody had first appeared, and the path he'd traveled during the storm with Elise by his side.

Would she bring Cody today so he could see his surprise?

Did he even want her to?

The answer hit him hard. In spite of her learning about his past and in spite of that nerve-rattling kiss, he still wanted—needed—to help Cody.

I honestly don't think I can get him ready for the IEP without your help.

Her desperate words had reinforced Jack's decision to spend the time and money necessary for today's surprise. But what if the effort were made in vain because Elise stepped over the line? Looked into his past. And then unsettled his world with that soul-shattering kiss.

He turned toward the porch, where he'd left the can of polyurethane that would help him complete the dresser. He'd thought Cody would enjoy assisting with the final action. Now he'd finish it on his own.

The platter of biscuits he'd prepared for breakfast remained untouched on the porch table, a jar of golden honey at its side and three coffee mugs nearby. He'd bought the Cocomotion specifically for Cody because he thought the kid would enjoy the warm treat on chilly mornings. Like today. Fall hit Alabama later than he'd expected, but there was a definite chill in the air. It'd be a great day for them to start with hot chocolate. He'd suspected Cody would like the whipped cream too.

His mind jolted with the memory of Elise, her mouth trimmed by the sweet white treat. And that memory naturally progressed to Elise tenderly stroking his jaw, her lips fusing with his, and nearly—*nearly*—making him forget his pain.

He shook the thought away. No reason to go there. Torture to his soul, and he didn't need any additional anguish.

A branch cracked, and he turned to see that he was no longer alone.

Elise walked slowly, timidly, toward the cabin with Cody by her side, his head tilted toward the ground.

She hesitated as she neared the porch, her shoulders low and her eyes pleading. "I…" she whispered. "I wasn't sure whether you would want us to come today, but Cody came to my cabin after breakfast with the hiking card in his hand." She shrugged. "I think he wanted to see you."

Cody glanced quickly up at Jack, then looked back down and slapped the card he clutched in one hand.

"I see." Jack didn't know how to speak to her, or what to say, after the uncomfortable interaction Friday night. But he was very glad to have Cody there.

"I told him you'd said something about a surprise for him." Elise looked toward the porch, and then at the dresser.

"I do, but it hasn't arrived yet."

Cody looked directly at Jack, his eyes sad and his mouth stretched into that hard straight line. He'd been disappointed at the football game when he'd expected the Mustang, but this wasn't like that.

"It won't be long, Cody. I promise. I've already heard from the guy bringing it. Probably be here within an hour or so."

Cody stuffed the flash card in his back pocket and moved his hands to his chest, directly in front of the vintage Mustang logo, to tap his fingers wildly.

"I like that logo, Cody," he said. "Old Mustangs are pretty cool, aren't they?"

His mouth tilted down at the corners, fingers tapped harder. Maybe talking about vintage cars wasn't the wisest thing after his disappointment at the field. But Jack's surprise should cheer him up.

"Tell you what, I made some biscuits and have plenty of that honey I know you like. And I got something special to go with it. How would you like hot chocolate with whipped cream?"

Cody's eyes brightened, and he peered past Jack to the platter of biscuits.

"You can go ahead and start on the biscuits and honey. I'll get the hot chocolate. Would you like whipped cream on top?"

Cody bobbed his head as he hurriedly climbed the porch steps, grabbed a plate and plopped three biscuits in the center. Then he pulled each one apart, so he could coat all sides with the honey.

Jack grinned at the kid. "The hot chocolate may not taste as sweet after all that sugar."

Cody looked up, his mouth stuffed with honey-covered biscuit. He chewed as best he could, with that much biscuit in his mouth. Then he pointed to his empty mug.

"Right. I'll get the hot chocolate." Jack figured the boy wouldn't mind the cocoa tasting a little bitter, as long as he had the treat.

Refusing to look at Elise, he entered the cabin and crossed to the kitchen, then pressed the button that would reheat the liquid in the hot chocolate maker.

"Jack."

He hadn't heard her follow him into the house, but he turned to find that she stood merely a few feet away. She wore a pale pink sweater, dark jeans and hiking boots, and she had her hair pulled up in one of those high ponytails that drew even more attention to the striking features of her face. "You can get the whipped cream out of the refrigerator if you want to help." The words came out sharp, but he couldn't help it. She shouldn't have looked into his past. "Might want to grab the marshmallows out of the pantry too, in case he'd rather have those."

Placing his hand on the side of the hot chocolate maker, he could still feel it stirring and heating the fluid. He'd known it wouldn't be ready yet, but he had wanted to put his attention on something other than the disarming female in his kitchen.

"Jack, I'm sorry." Her whispered words were delivered very near his left ear.

He refused to turn toward her and instead watched for the machine to stop.

"I pried into your past, and I shouldn't have done that. I'm very sorry, Jack, and I'm asking you to forgive me."

The machine was never going to quit.

He heard her sigh, and part of him wanted to tell her not to worry, everything would be okay. But everything wouldn't, not between them, because she made him want the impossible. So he kept his attention on the Co-comotion.

"I may have gone about getting the information in the wrong manner, but I think God led me to learn about you, about how talented you are, because we need you, Jack. Cody needs you, and what you can do."

That got his attention. "I'm helping Cody."

"You are," she agreed softly, "but he needs something that, I'm fairly certain, you are the only one that can provide. Something to help him find a new family, Jack."

He hadn't wanted to look at her, but he couldn't help himself. He turned, leaned against the counter and let their eyes connect. Hers held hope. His, he suspected, held accusation. "What does he need, Elise?"

Her lower lip trembled, but Jack wouldn't let himself worry why.

"What does he need?" he repeated.

"He needs for families to see him the way we do, for folks to understand what he's gone through and want to help him, love him—" she paused, swallowed "—give him a forever home with people he can depend on."

"I thought you said that if we could get him out of his shell, have him communicate and interact with others, *that* would help his chances of adoption."

She ran a finger along the counter's edge, looked away from Jack. Whatever she was about to say, he'd wager he didn't want to hear it.

"That *will* help his chances, but people still need to *see* him. Not only Cody but all of the other kids at Willow's Haven." She stopped watching her finger on the counter and drew her eyes toward him. "They're currently maxed out, Jack. They can't take any more children, but there are a lot of kids like Cody, or actually, not even in as good of a position as Cody. They don't have a children's home. They don't have any home. They are bounced from house to house, family to family or orphanage to orphanage, and they all need the same thing—someone to want them. Someone to love them. Just like Cody."

The conviction in her tone reminded Jack

of himself, when he described the reason he had to make a particular film, tell a specific story. Because it called to him. Because it pricked his heart. "What is it you want me to do, Elise?"

"Savvy talked to a large children's home in Atlanta about how they find families for the kids there, and she learned that the best way they've found to get people to understand how precious the kids are and how much they need a family is…" She turned her head to the side, as if dreading his response, and then she finally blurted, "To create a video of the children."

Jack's pulse dropped.

Her eyes widened, and she must have taken his lack of response as a sign to proceed at a rapid pace, because she rattled the remainder of her request. "They wouldn't show it until Christmas. It's called a Christmas appeal. It'd be shown at all of the churches, and it's a way for people to see the children without the kids having to travel around from church to church, since that really isn't good for them, since they need stability, and the stability factor of church for them is to stay at the only church they've known since they moved to Willow's Haven."

Jack's head shook on its own accord. What was she thinking? But she didn't acknowledge his response, just continued with her unbelievable request.

"Savvy said she didn't know any videographers, and I know that you're well above that type of thing, as far as what you've done before, but I also know that you would be the absolute best shot that they would have for all of the kids in the home—and Cody—to have a chance at a real family." She cleared her throat. "And I'm certain God brought you here for this, Jack. Probably for other reasons too, but definitely for this. It's meant for you. Your films have been so inspiring, the kind that pull at your heart and never let go. They remind us of how we should be, letting God lead us every day, following His will, and I know you're the one meant to make this video—"

"Absolutely not."

Elise knew he'd still be mad at her, had braced herself for it, through every painstaking step of the walk with Cody from Willow's Haven. But she hadn't anticipated him refusing so vehemently to make the video.

Couldn't he see that's why God brought him here? To help Cody and to help the kids at

Willow's Haven? Yes, he was angry with her, but he shouldn't let the fact that she'd snooped into his past stop him from helping the kids who needed him, especially the one beside him now, working on the dresser.

She watched him talk to Cody and find a way to interact with the boy even though Cody never uttered a word. If she didn't know any better, she'd say they were father and son.

JJ. She recalled the photo of Jack's boy, merely a year younger than Cody when he died. She had no doubt losing the boy—losing all of his family—had damaged Jack's faith. She'd known people who turned away from God, even blamed Him, during times of trouble.

But this was Jack Simon. The faith director. His entire career had been spent proclaiming the goodness of God. And his last movie at the box office had calmed her distressed soul, given her the strength to keep trusting God to guide her through the storm in spite of her pain.

How could *Jack Simon* say no to helping these children, specifically this boy? He cared about Cody. She could see it in the way he looked at him, hear it in the way he spoke to him, like now.

Jack eyed the instructions on the side of a can of clear satin polyurethane. "Okay, Cody, from what this says, we're supposed to brush a thin coat evenly on the wood to protect it from water marks, household cleaners and everyday wear. And then our dresser will be finished." He placed the yellow can on a workbench, grabbed a screwdriver and pried the lid off. "We don't need to stir this or shake it, because that'll make bubbles in the top coat."

Elise watched as Cody peered around Jack's arm to see the thick liquid in the can. He handed Cody a brush. "You want to get started?"

Cody stepped near the dresser but didn't make any effort to dip the brush in the can. Instead, he ran the bristles against his opposite palm and stretched his mouth into that familiar thin flat line.

Elise noticed his hesitation and knew that he wasn't comfortable with the assigned task. Then he confirmed her suspicion by placing the brush on top of the dresser and moving his hands to his chest to start his rapid finger thumping.

He'd been excited about every aspect that had been involved with completing the dresser. But now that he'd reached the final step, he looked wary, with reluctance and in-decision etched clearly on his face.

And she wasn't the only one who noticed.

Jack wrapped an arm around him and leaned in toward the boy. The image of father and son was so prominent that Elise would be surprised if Jack didn't sense it too. A hard lump formed in her throat. How could Jack not help Cody find a family again? Have a father again?

"Cody," he said, his voice low and steady, "Elise and I know you can do this. We have total faith in you."

Elise and I. Warmth flooded her, because she liked being included. She wanted Cody to know that she believed in him, and that she wanted to help him.

Still leaning toward Cody, Jack pointed to the dresser. "It's the last step, and then I'll have a one-of-a-kind piece of furniture, a Jack-and-Cody original." He smiled. "But I want you involved with the final step. Be-cause I know you can do it. And Elise and I will help you."

Cody's throat bobbed with a thick swallow as he locked gazes with his mentor and then reached for the brush.

Jack grabbed a brush and then extended

another one toward Elise. "You are going to help, right?"

She took the brush. "*I* am."

Jack had ignored the jibe from Elise about the brush. He also managed to apply the coat of polyurethane with the two of them without conversing with her, touching her or anything else that had to do with her.

He was still mad at Elise. First, she'd gone meddling into his past, and then she'd tried to guilt him into making a film. No, it wasn't the type of large-scale production, full-length movie that he typically directed, but it would still be a film. And Willow's Haven was a Christian children's home; therefore, the video would undeniably be God-focused.

Jack wasn't doing God any more favors.

Even if it meant helping Cody.

Besides, once his surprise arrived, he believed the kid might find a reason to be happy again and to start interacting more. Maybe enough to satisfy that IEP team Elise was so concerned about.

Before today, she'd claimed that getting him to interact would be the best step toward finding him a home. But suddenly, after discovering Jack directed films, she'd decided having a video produced would be his best chance.

Odd how that all changed after she'd learned about his past.

He suddenly recalled the first time he saw her, crying out in the woods, her anguished sobs resonating through him. The vision had consumed his thoughts for days. And nights. He'd worried about her, even before he learned that she was real. She'd been so pained. So grief-stricken. Her cries calling to his heart, his spirit.

What had happened in *her* past that had so thoroughly tortured *her* soul?

Jack didn't want to know. He didn't.

Soon she'd leave. And then he wouldn't have to see anyone who knew about his profession. No one trying to guilt him into doing something he didn't want to do. She may have found out about his pain, but he didn't want to learn about hers. That would make him care more. And he didn't want to care at all.

"What are we going to do next?" she asked, as he hammered the lid back onto the polyurethane can.

He'd thought the guy would've brought his surprise by now. He glanced at his watch. "I had expected…"

A rumble echoed in the distance, but this wasn't thunder. Jack grinned as the sound got louder, and the large truck made its way up the winding hill that led to Jack's house. The gravel drive ended at his garage, behind the house, so he motioned for Cody to follow him. "This is my surprise. Come on, I think you're going to like it."

Elise walked on the other side of Cody as they moved around the side of the house, and Jack let her take a few steps ahead of him because he wanted to see her reaction too.

The guy driving the truck held up a hand as he cleared the trees and started closer to the garage.

"What is it?" she asked.

Jack hadn't expected him to bring an enclosed truck, but that was even better. They'd have to wait a moment before the unveil. "You'll see."

They stopped walking when the guy parked the truck and climbed out.

"You Mr. Simon?" He had a thick Cajun drawl, which made sense, since Jack had located his surprise in a small town in South Louisiana.

"I am." Jack stepped toward the man, and the guy extended a clipboard.

"Everything's paid for," the guy said, "but I'm sure you knew dat." He grinned broadly. "Gotta tell you, I was a little nervous hauling it. Never had anything—"

Jack held up a hand. "It's a surprise." He nodded toward Cody, whose fingers were thumping at a feverish pace as he stared at the back of the truck.

"Aw, gotcha." He looked to Cody. "Well, *chère*, let me tell you, you're gonna be mighty happy with what your daddy done brought ya."

Jack noticed Elise started to say something, but he shook his head. No need to correct the guy. He'd assumed Jack was Cody's dad. Nothing wrong with that. A logical assumption.

The Cajun moved to the back of the truck, and Elise, Cody and Jack followed.

"You want them to close der eyes?" the Cajun offered.

Jack liked this guy. "Why not?"

"Seriously?" Elise asked, but then she looked at Cody, and he'd stopped tapping his fingers and moved his palms over his eyes. "Oh, all right, then." She slid her eyes closed.

The guy motioned for Jack to come help

him, and Jack jumped up the ramp to view the hidden treasure inside.

"It's even better than the pictures."

"I shore ain't seen one any prettier."

The Cajun climbed in and put the vehicle in Neutral, then the two of them backed it slowly down the ramp near the garage entrance, where they'd have to push it in. Jack hadn't wanted one that would run. What would be the fun in that? This way he and Cody could work on it together.

"Okay," he said, as the Cajun backed away and placed his hands on his hips to watch the show. "You can open your eyes."

Elise was the first to drop her hands, and then drop her jaw. "Jack! Oh, my. It's…so beautiful."

Cody still held his palms in place, and a fragment of fear pinched at Jack. What if he didn't like surprises? What if this actually made him worse instead of better?

"It's okay, Cody," Elise coaxed in a soothing tone. "Really, I think you're going to like it." She put a hand on his right forearm and gently guided it away, and then she did the same with the left.

Cody kept his eyes closed tight, his head

turned to the side and his mouth cringing. He honestly didn't want to look.

Jack moved beside the boy who had captured his heart and wrapped an arm around him. "Cody, this isn't anything bad. It's very good, in fact, and I would really like for you to open your eyes. I wanted to get something for us to work on together, besides furniture. And I think you're going to want to see it."

The eyes remained shut.

"Please, Cody," Jack rasped. "You can trust me. This isn't anything that will hurt. Open your eyes." He looked to Elise, saw tears trickling free. "Come on, Cody, I want you to see the surprise. Trust me," he repeated.

Cody warily opened his eyes. And started to clap. And smile. And laugh. While Elise continued to cry, and Jack squeezed the boy's shoulders.

"I take it you like the surprise, then?" Jack asked, relief flooding through him. "It needs an engine, and a few other things, but nothing we can't handle together."

Cody turned toward Jack, wrapped his arms around him and squeezed. While Jack fought the enormous lump in his throat.

Then he said, "Do you know what this one is, Cody? It's a—"

"It's a…a…" Cody stuttered, "a 1964 ½, the very first Mustang they made."

Elise gasped, while Jack turned toward the child still chattering away.

"They…they called it a ½-year model because they released it five months before the normal start of the 1965 production year."

The truck driver slapped his hand against his thigh. "Well, that boy you got there is pretty smart, ain't he?"

Jack swallowed, squeezed Cody's shoulders again and didn't overly mind that this man assumed Cody was his son. "Yes, he is."

Chapter Eight

"And it took us three days to put the new crate engine in, Mark. Then it only took an hour to replace the alternator. We've still got to put in the radiator and the water pump. And Mr. Jack is going to pick up the new belts and hoses as soon as the store in Stockville calls. We had to order them custom." Cody motioned for his cabin counselor and the other boys from his cabin to follow him to the front of the car, where he grinned as he pointed to the engine-in-progress. "Look, Konrad, isn't it cool?"

Elise listened to Cody effectively answer each question while she and Jack merely watched, amazed at the transition that had occurred over the past week. Jack knew that Cody had been through intensive therapy with

Elise, but still…he'd come so far, and Jack was beyond thrilled to have been a small part of it.

Elise stated the obvious. "He's going to do great on that IEP. It's only three days away, you know."

Jack continued cleaning up the work area. He returned a socket wrench to the appropriate slot in its case. "I think you're right."

This was what she'd prayed for, to hear Cody speak again and to see him interact with other kids. As intelligent as she'd expected, Cody could handle his own in any conversation, though he'd always offer more information than was actually needed. However, none of his newfound friends seemed to mind. "He'll be mainstreamed in the school system, I have no doubt. And then my work here will be done."

He'd had a screwdriver in his hand, but he stopped moving toward the large red toolbox and looked at Elise. "So you'll head back to Birmingham, then."

"That's the plan." She attempted to keep the sadness from her voice, but failed. "Jack, I know I told you that his chances of being adopted would be greater if he could interact with others, and I still believe that's true."

"Why do I hear a 'but' coming?" He dropped the screwdriver into a drawer in the red toolbox.

Since that night in the rain, he'd spoken to her only when necessary, and she didn't blame him. She had snooped into his past. Elise could have told him that she'd done it because she had to make sure he was safe to be around Cody, which would have been true. However, that wasn't the only reason. She'd also simply wanted to know more about Jack.

But in three days, Cody would probably sail through that IEP interview and be placed in the nondisabled schoolroom. Then she'd return home. And no one would get this man to accomplish what Elise knew he needed to do.

"*But* I also think that his chances would be even greater if they could 'see' him interacting with other kids, watch him talk about the Mustang, hear him laugh. Potential adoptive families will be told that Cody is autistic. Yes, they will learn that he can interact with others and that he has been mainstreamed at school, assuming he is—"

"He will be," Jack interjected.

She smiled, grateful for his faith that Cody would succeed and also grateful that he'd purchased the spark—in the form of a vintage automobile—that Cody needed to finally break out of his shell.

"I believe he will too. But even if a family is told how great he's doing, they will also have to be told that he is autistic. And without seeing him, they won't realize what that means. They could never fully understand how wonderful he is." She moistened her lips. "You could do that for him, Jack. You could let people see him the way we do. And who knows? You might also help more of these kids get adopted, if you were willing to use the talent God gave you. You have to believe that's what *He* wants for you."

Jack slammed the lid of the toolbox, clenched his jaw and turned to glare angrily at Elise. "God took my family. I'm not concerned with what *He* wants."

Elise had suspected how he felt, but she'd never heard him blatantly place the blame of losing his family on God. She was thankful the kids were too absorbed in Cody's dynamic description of the car to hear Jack's proclamation. She didn't want to remind him that he needed to watch what he said in front of the eleven-and twelve-year-old boys from Cody's cabin. She'd been surprised he'd even agreed to let Cody bring Mark, his counselor, and his cabinmates. But she'd learned something else about Jack Simon over the past week.

He wouldn't let Cody down.

Which was why she asked again.

"Okay. So don't do it because of God. Do it because of *Cody*! You know he needs a family. He deserves one. And a video could make all the difference, Jack, especially if it were produced by you."

Cody laughed at something Mark said and then shoved the counselor with his shoulder. He was so happy now, and Elise wanted the world, particularly parents who might adopt the boy, to see it.

"Do it for Cody, Jack."

He'd also homed in on the scene before them, and how ecstatic the lad looked talking with his friends and chattering about the many plans they had for the car. "It'd make an emotional video."

His words were barely audible, but Elise heard. And inwardly celebrated. No, he hadn't come around to making movies for God again, but this was definitely a step in the right direction. And, even though she'd promised herself she wouldn't fall into the same old trap, she knew she couldn't return to Birmingham without knowing that she'd helped Cody as much as she could. And without knowing she'd helped Jack as much as she could too. "You're going to do it, aren't you?" she asked softly.

He frowned. "I guess I am."

Elise didn't stop the impulse. She wrapped both arms around him in a hug. "Thank you, Jack."

He stiffened in her embrace, then stepped away from her completely. "I'm doing it for Cody. He deserves the best chance at a family, and I want to give him that."

He could've punched her in the stomach, and it'd have hurt less. "Right. Well, I'm glad. I want him to have the best chance too."

Jack couldn't have planned two more perfect days for filming. Though it was already the second week of November, the temperature had hovered between sixty-eight and seventy-one while he'd been filming the kids.

It'd felt odd at first, visiting the children's home and having so many people surrounding him, when all he'd wanted was to get away from folks completely. But this would help Cody have a better chance at adoption, so Jack suffered through the process.

Not that he actually suffered. The children were adorable. And the bond they shared with each other over their similar circumstances was profound and easily captured on film. He couldn't wait to get back to the cabin and start going over the footage. Jack had no doubt that if a couple were even remotely interested in the potential of fostering or adopting, they would be smitten by these kids.

They sure grabbed Jack's heart, especially Cody, who proudly introduced each and every kid at Willow's Haven to "Amazing Mr. Jack." The first time he'd said it, Jack had felt uncomfortable. He didn't deserve such adoration from a child who wasn't his. But by the last time Cody said it, he'd decided he liked hearing it, and he sure enjoyed watching Cody when he said it, always hugging Jack at the mere mention of his name.

Elise had accompanied him for each shot, and Jack had fought the impulse to stare as she interacted with the children, bringing out their best qualities, whether that be the way they laughed, or the way they talked, or the way they loved. She had a natural rapport with children, and with adults, if Jack considered the fact that she kept penetrating his own boundaries for getting close. Even when he attempted to push her away, she still managed to infiltrate his emotions, cause him to want to do more, *be* more. And unfortunately, she made him want to do that...with her.

Tomorrow. Tomorrow, she and the IEP team would meet and discuss Cody, and then they would interview the boy, and they'd see how he deserved every school benefit that could be afforded to him. He'd be placed in a classroom with his peers, probably many of the boys he'd proclaimed as "his very best friends" over the past week, and then, once churches viewed the video and saw how amazing he was, he'd be adopted.

Cody would have a loving family, Elise would return to Birmingham...and Jack would be alone.

His throat pinched, but he swallowed past it. Tomorrow couldn't get here quick enough. He needed Elise and Cody to be out of his life, so he could keep from feeling so much.

A little girl, probably around four years old, ran after Elise as they made their way toward the trail to leave Willow's Haven.

"Miss Elise! You forgot my hug!" She smiled broadly as she puffed out small breaths at the end of her endearing gallop from her cabin.

Elise crouched down to catch her. "How could I forget your hug?" She smiled, hugged the child with one of those cheek-rubbing actions that prominently displayed the immense affection she had for the little girl.

Jack was glad he still had his camera in hand, because he caught the tender moment on film. Elise would make an incredible mother. And an incredible wife.

He blinked past the thought and squinted to continue viewing the exquisite scene before him.

"I love you big as the sky, Miss Elise," the tiny child said, "to the moon and back."

"I love you too, Naomi." Elise kissed her cheek and touched one of her pigtails. "I'll see you when I get back from my walk with Cody and his friends, okay?"

The little girl frowned. "Can't I go with you for the walk? Please?"

Savvy had started toward them, presumably to steer Naomi back toward her cabin. Elise looked to her and asked, "Can Naomi join us?"

Naomi put her palms together beneath her chin, the symbol of prayer—or in this case, begging—and Savvy laughed. "Yes, that's fine."

Then the little girl turned and squeezed Elise while Jack caught the interaction on film.

"Perfect." He nodded, satisfied that he'd obtained plenty of footage to work with, except for what would probably be his favorite thing to film. "So, have you got some friends that want to go see the car, Cody?"

Cody pointed to the crew of boys surrounding him. "I have five. Alanus, Jeremiah, Ryan, Brooks and Konrad." He pointed to each youngster as he said the name. "They've seen it before, but they want to see it again for the camera."

"Sounds great. Let's go."

The boys led the way, with Cody excitedly telling them all about his trip through the woods the first day and how he found Amazing Mr. Jack working on furniture.

"And I didn't even know he knew anything about cars. Because he never told me when we were working on the furniture," Cody said, his group well ahead of Jack, Elise and Naomi. "But he's pretty good with cars. He doesn't know everything, but when we don't know something, we can find it in one of my books.

Or sometimes on the internet. And there's always the YouTube videos."

This introduced a discussion of their favorite things to watch on YouTube.

Elise laughed faintly.

"What is it?" Jack had done his best not to get close to her since he'd learned she had invaded his privacy by poking into his past. And since she'd shown him how much he had missed with that kiss. But most likely, she'd be leaving tomorrow. So he didn't think it'd hurt to ask her what he wanted to know.

"All of those days I've walked through the woods either on my own or with Cody, it seemed a lonely place. Beautiful, but still lonely."

"Can I pick up some of these to show Miss Savvy?" Naomi asked, pointing to the gold and red leaves that lined the path.

"Sure." Elise patted Naomi's back before she skipped toward a multicolored red, gold and green leaf.

Jack wanted to hear what else Elise had planned to say. "It seemed lonely?"

She smiled as Naomi held up the leaf and then raced ahead to some bright orange ones in the distance. "Yeah. I mean, I always felt God here. I still do…" She paused, but Jack wasn't going to head into another God discussion; it only ended with her being disappointed and him getting angry. So she continued, "But today, watching Cody lead his friends down the path and now talking with Naomi about leaves and…" She nodded as the little girl showed her more of her finds, and didn't finish her sentence.

"And what, Elise?"

She shoved her hands in her jeans pockets, looked away from him and said softly, "And spending time with you, Jack. This *isn't* lonely. This is making a memory. And I'm going to treasure it forever."

There was something about this woman. No matter what he did to try to keep her from reaching his heart, touching his soul, she managed to find a way. He wanted to tell her he'd treasure the memory too. But that would open doors that needed to remain closed. She couldn't know that he thought about her even when they weren't together, that he dreamed about her and wondered what life could be like…if he could trust God not to take everything he loved away again.

Everything he loved. Why had Cody and Elise, and even Willow's Haven, filled his thoughts when he said those words?

"Mr. Amazing Jack!" Cody called. "Someone is here!"

"Let's see who it is!" Naomi clapped as she dropped her leaves and ran the short distance to the end of the trail.

Laughing, Elise picked up the discarded leaves. "She'll want these later, I'm sure." Then she glanced at Jack, and it was all he could do to keep walking toward the end of the trail, instead of stopping, hauling her into his arms and begging her not to leave tomorrow.

And then he'd—

"Mr. Amazing Jack! It's your friend!"

"My friend?" Jack's thoughts of Elise were cut short because he was certain none of his "friends" knew where he lived now.

"Were you expecting someone?" Elise increased her pace to match Jack's as he strode through the remainder of the woods to see who he'd find waiting at the end of the trail.

"I want to meet Mr. Jack's friend." Naomi ran toward Cody and the boys, all standing near a black car parked beside Jack's house.

Jack didn't recognize the car, but he easily recognized the man standing next to it and talking to Cody.

"I completely agree," Vincent said to Cody,

"there isn't anything much more special than a 1964 ½ Mustang."

"I can show it to you. Do you want to see it? I can tell you what all me and Mr. Amazing Jack have done so far, but we have a lot more to do. But I can tell you about that too." Cody smiled when he saw Jack. "Look, your friend is here!"

"I see that." He looked at the man who truly had been one of his closest friends for over a decade. "How are you, Vincent?"

"Actually, I was going to ask you that, since how I am, and how a lot of other people are, basically depends on you." Vincent wore a black cable-knit sweater with jeans, quite a contrast from the suits he typically preferred, but he still sported his herringbone newsboy cap that he'd always claimed made him look like a successful Hollywood agent...even before he actually was a successful Hollywood agent.

"Cody, why don't you take the guys into the garage and show them the badges and wheels that came in this morning?"

Elise and Naomi stood a few feet away, so Jack added, "Elise, would you mind taking Naomi into the garage too, so I can talk to Vincent? It won't take long."

"O-kay." Clearly confused, she scooped up Naomi and carried her toward the garage.

As soon as they were out of earshot, Jack turned toward his agent. "How did you find me?"

"Now, you know your mom has always had a soft spot for me. I told her I needed to see you, and not only did she give me the address, but she also promised to send me one of those coconut pies she makes that I love so much."

"I thought she understood I didn't want company." He'd been *very* clear about that.

"Yeah, she mentioned it, but she also said that she was worried about you and thought you could use a visit from a friend." He grinned. "So I offered to make the trip, in case things weren't going so great in the woods."

"Mighty thoughtful of you."

Vincent grinned. "Though it doesn't seem as rough as I'd anticipated. Very pretty out here. Reminds me of what an amazing job God did with Creation, don't you think?"

Jack frowned. "Vincent, tell me. Why *are* you here? And don't say it's because my mother asked you to come."

"Well, for one, to make sure my friend is okay. And I'm glad to see you aren't holed up like Tom Hanks in *Cast Away*, living in a cave and talking to a volleyball named Wilson."

Vincent had always been able to make him smile; now was no exception.

"If you had shown up a month ago, that'd have been closer to the picture." Jack recalled the way he looked the first day when Cody and Elise had shown up at his cabin, not all that different from Tom Hanks in the notable movie.

"I figured. I'm glad I waited to come, then. It's good to see you around people. Around kids again. And, I might add, a very pretty lady."

Jack didn't want to discuss the woman who would most likely be leaving tomorrow. "What is it, Vincent? Why are you really here?"

"I'm here to tell you that Roland *wasn't* blowing smoke. The breach of contract suit is in the attorney's hands, and if you don't show up for all scheduled appearances in the press junket, beginning with the screening the day after Thanksgiving, it'll be in the hands of the court."

Jack ran his hand through his hair, thought about the press junkets of the past and how he'd gone to every event, no matter how big or how small, to benefit the studio. He'd given them great pictures and his total support, right up until that plane went down. "They have a solid film, Vincent. It'll stand on its own, and you and I both know word of mouth is the best advertising there is. They don't need me."

"See now, that's where we're gonna have to agree to disagree, because I know if the public doesn't see you at this film, hear you talk about the movie, why you made it and what it means to you, then they are going to think you don't care. And trust me, Jack, then they won't care."

Even though Jack feared he was right, it didn't change his stance. "You want me to tell people why I made the film? You want me to get up in front of a crowd, or sit in front of a camera crew at a talk show, and explain that the idea for *Finding Home* came about when we finally found JJ, after he'd gotten lost when we were filming in Prague? You expect me to talk about the first time I lost my son, when I know it will only lead to the inevitable questions about how I lost him— and Laney, and AmyJo, and Sadie—on the day of my last movie's premiere? Because you *know* they will ask, Vincent. And you *know* what I'll say."

"That God turned His back on you." Vincent released a deep breath. "Listen, Jack, I know you were hurting—that you're still hurting—but I still believe God is in control. Life isn't always about happy endings, except the final ending, the one that matters. You'll be with your family again, Jack, and—" He swallowed, shook his head. "I know this isn't what you want to hear, but I have to admit that when I got here and saw all those kids coming to the cabin, and then the little girl and the lady, I said a prayer of thanks."

"A prayer of thanks?"

"That God was obviously blessing you again and that you were finally starting to live again. I've missed you, Jack. Lots of people have. We care about you. And Damascus Entertainment *does* need you to promote this picture. It is a solid film, like you said, and therefore it needs your backing. It needs to be seen by Christians and non-Christians worldwide. It's another chance for you to make a difference in a very big way."

"I can't do it, Vincent. This—" he waved his hand toward the garage and the crowd of people in it "—this isn't God blessing me. It's me, helping a little boy get adopted. And as soon as that's done, I will be on my own here.

Just like you expected. Tom Hanks, but with no volleyball." He expected Vincent to smile at that, or crack another joke.

Instead, he looked like he was going to get sick. "You could ruin all of us, Jack," he said softly. "Are you willing to do that? Because that's not the Jack Simon I know."

Jack started to tell him that the Jack Simon he knew died the day that plane went down. But before he could get started, Elise called to him from the garage.

"Jack, they're getting a little restless. Could you come film them before they tear the garage apart? They're pretty fascinated with your tools."

"Sure." He nodded at his friend. "It was good to see you, Vincent. Sorry I couldn't give you the answer you wanted."

"So all of the ten percenters, the ones you always cared about more than any other director in the industry, you're okay with that many people losing a year's pay?"

"I've got to go film these kids," Jack bit out, walking away.

Elise exited the garage with Naomi on her hip. "She's got to use the bathroom. Can she use yours inside?"

In spite of his frustrations from the visit

with Vincent, Jack managed a gentle smile for the little girl. "Sure, Naomi."

She grinned back, and then Elise continued past him and Vincent, while Jack tried not to think about how many people he'd be disappointing and focused on filming Cody and his friends.

Chapter Nine

Elise held the cabin door open for Naomi, who darted out and then practically ran down the front steps. "Be careful."

"Yes, ma'am." Naomi waved as she ran past the man leaning against the black car. "Hey, Mr. Jack's friend."

He smiled, a nice, pleasant smile. "Hey to you."

Naomi rushed into the garage, while Elise also greeted the fellow who didn't seem in any hurry to leave. "Hello."

"Hello." He chanced a glance to the garage, where Elise could see Jack behind the camera shooting the boys as they took turns in the driver's seat, and as Naomi climbed into the backseat. "It's Elise, isn't it?"

She didn't see any reason she shouldn't talk

to the man. Jack had wanted to speak to him in private, but he hadn't acted as though the guy was any sort of threat. In fact, she suspected they were friends. "Yes, that's correct."

He nodded. "So, I see Jack's filming again here, even if it is on a lower scale than what he's used to."

Elise wasn't sure what to say, but she knew Jack wouldn't want this man broadcasting his career to everyone around town. "I'm pretty sure I'm the only one who knows what Jack did before. He's keeping it low-key."

The man slid two fingers across his forehead and tilted the gray cap away from his face. "But you know that he's Jack Simon. You know what he did—what he does for a living. You know how important he is to the industry, particularly when it involves films of faith."

Elise nodded. "I do."

He slid his lower lip to the side as though debating how much to say. And Elise wondered whether Jack would be okay with her hearing it.

"I should probably head into the garage too." She smiled politely and started to leave.

"A lot of people are going to be really hurting if he doesn't show up for his press junket. Did he tell you that? In all honesty, I'm okay without a year's pay, but the other ten percenters...well, I'd say they'll have a blue Christmas unless Jack shows up for that screening the day after Thanksgiving. And every other scheduled appearance."

She didn't understand, but the thought of people hurting at Christmas bothered her, especially if it was for something that Jack still had time to correct. "What is a ten percenter?"

"Folks like me, his agent, and all of the director's team, as they say. We're called that because we get ten percent of a director's earnings on a project. So if he forfeits his pay, we don't get paid. Or, in this case, if he is in breach of contract, we don't get paid."

"Breach of contract?" Elise wasn't familiar with any of this.

"As the director of the film, he's contractually required to attend all activities on the film's press junket. His first event is the screening on the day after Thanksgiving. Then he has several more scheduled before Christmas Day, when the film is set to release. Unless they postpone it again, since Jack isn't on board."

"And if he doesn't attend?" She wanted to make sure she understood correctly.

"Roland Mooreland, the studio exec, already has the papers in the attorney's hands. If Jack doesn't show up, we won't get paid." He sighed heavily, looked toward the garage, where Jack had moved to the front of the car to film under the hood. "This isn't merely about getting paid. He's the best I've ever seen at bringing God to the big screen, and I don't know how long it'll take for another director to learn how to do that anywhere near as well as Jack. He's got a gift."

"I agree. His movies mean a lot to everyone. They've…meant a lot to me."

He knuckled his hat and nodded in agreement. "His heart and his faith—or at least the faith he used to have—are conveyed right there, on-screen, for the world to see. God has used Jack in a big way, and to see him turn his back on the Lord, or blame Him for what happened…" His jaw twitched, and Elise wondered if he fought tears. "We just don't need to lose a man like Jack in the industry."

"And if he doesn't do the press junket things?"

"He'll never work in LA again. And the Christian film industry will take such a hit, it might as well be nonexistent. Jack Simon *is* the faith director. Without him, there's really nothing else out there that glorifies God."

The hood of the Mustang snapped closed, and Jack suddenly peered directly at them.

"Looks like I've been caught," Vincent said, tipping his hat to his friend. "Listen, Elise, if there's anything you can do to help me out, let me know. We need him at that screening. And we need him at everything else too." He handed her his business card.

Elise slid the card into her jeans pocket. "I don't think I'll do any good, but I'll try."

"Can't ask for more than that, I suppose. Unless you'll pray too." He winked, and Elise found herself smiling.

"Oh, don't worry. I'll do plenty of that."

"Kind of suspected you would." He turned to leave but then noticed that Jack had been summoned by the kids to look at something in the car. "Elise?"

"Yes?"

"Where are all of these kids from?"

"Willow's Haven. It's a children's home a short distance away, down that path." She motioned to the trail. "Jack is making a video that we're going to use at area churches to try to find foster homes and adoptive families for the kids."

"Jack's going to church again?" He didn't disguise his surprise.

"Oh, no, he isn't," she clarified. "And I'll be honest, I kind of guilted him into it. He's grown very close to one of the boys, Cody, and I told him this would be Cody's best shot at getting a family. I didn't lie. I do think it is."

Vincent grinned. "I believe you. And you know what else?"

"What's that?"

"I'm fairly certain that God isn't done with Jack Simon yet."

Elise watched him climb in his car and drive away, giving her another tip of his hat before heading down the gravel drive. Then she turned to see Jack kneeling near the front of the Mustang. They'd lifted the hood once more, and he had his camera tilted up to capture something she couldn't see on the other side. He must have liked what he saw, because she could tell that he smiled as he filmed.

Several of the kids were sitting inside the car when she walked past to see what held Jack's attention.

It was Cody, holding Naomi.

"And what's that?" She pointed to something under the hood.

"That's the alternator."

"What's that?" She pointed to something else.

"That's the water pump."

The tiny girl must have thought "water pump" was something funny, because she started a belly giggle that made Cody laugh too. Then he tweaked Naomi's nose, and she leaned her forehead to touch his, then laughed some more.

"Oh, my. They are so beautiful together."

Jack finished catching the shot, then stood beside her. "I don't know how anyone wouldn't want to adopt them, do you? And look at Cody...he'll be an amazing big brother." His words were filled with gruff tenderness.

She nodded, dreading the moment that she had to tell them goodbye. "Thank you for making the video, Jack. I know that will help so many of these kids, including those two."

"That's what we want, right?" He said the words, but he sounded as though he might be thinking the same thing as Elise, that it would be very sad to have days that didn't include these kids.

"Elise?" Savvy's voice called from outside the garage. "You in there?"

Glad for the diversion, Elise started out. She

didn't want to think about leaving after that IEP meeting tomorrow. Didn't want to think about leaving Cody. Or Jack. "Yes?"

"Hey, I tried to call you, but you didn't answer." Savvy grinned. "Did you leave your phone in your cabin?"

Elise couldn't remember where she had it last, and then she recalled sitting it on the counter in Jack's house when she'd taken Naomi to the bathroom. "I left it inside." She pointed to his cabin. "Did you need me?"

"I just wanted to let the kids know that the Cutter Dude Ranch has the horses ready for one last ride before winter and invited all of the Willow's Haven kids to come today. We've got a bus on the way to pick them up."

The boys and Naomi exited the garage in a rush.

"We're going to ride horses?" Naomi clapped her hands together. "Really?"

Savvy laughed. "Really, but you need to get to Willow's Haven and grab a jacket. It'll probably be dark before we get back, and when it gets dark, it gets cold."

"Come on, let's go get jackets and ride horses!" Cody rounded up the troop and led the way.

"You want to come too, Elise? You can if

you want." Savvy laughed as Cody stretched out a hand for a high five as he passed.

"Will you come ride horses too, Miss Elise?" Naomi asked, her sweet smile almost making Elise want to go.

But this might be her last full day at Willow's Haven. And her final chance to talk to Jack.

"I don't think so," she said, more to Naomi than to Savvy, "but I'll see you when you get back, okay?"

"Would you read me a bedtime story?"

"I would love to." Elise enjoyed spending time with the little girl. Of course, all of the adults at Willow's Haven enjoyed spending time with Naomi. She was so animated and happy. Every counselor, at one time or another, had read a bedtime story or two to the child.

Obviously delighted with Elise's response, Naomi ran toward her, arms wide, and Elise, used to this reaction, crouched down and accepted the heart-melting hug.

"I love you, Miss Elise. Big as the sky, to the moon and back."

Did any words ever sound sweeter? Elise swallowed, glad that she'd get to have at least one more of these hugs tonight, after that bed-time story. "I love you too."

Naomi released her, then ran toward Savvy. "Okay, let's go ride horses, Miss Savvy."

"Let's go." Savvy took her hand. "I'll see you tonight, Elise."

"See you tonight." She waited for them to start down the trail and then turned toward the man now standing on the porch. He wore a flannel shirt rolled up at the elbows, similar to the one he had on the first day she'd seen him when he'd sported that horrid beard. Odd, how the flannel shirt seemed to suit him in either capacity, rugged and bearded or clean shaven.

Always heart-stopping.

Would she ever meet another guy who made her feel as much as she felt toward Jack? Would she ever meet one so complicated, tormented, impossibly stubborn?

Exactly the type of guy she shouldn't want to meet.

But Jack was so much more than that. He was also a man whose faith had been challenged and needed to be made whole again. His heart had been broken and needed to heal. His trust had been tested, not his trust in man, but his trust in God.

Elise was certain she'd witnessed the "old

Jack" over the past few days, as he interacted with Cody and the other children. He'd been at home behind the camera, and she'd witnessed him laughing on more than one occasion. She'd also seen him cry once, or she'd thought she saw a tear slide down his cheek when he filmed the kids having the afternoon devotional yesterday at the fire pit.

That Jack didn't need to fade away into oblivion. Like Vincent said, God wasn't finished with him yet. He'd sounded so sure.

And Elise was too. But how could she convince him to have true faith and trust God again in spite of the past pain?

He didn't waste time asking what he wanted. As soon as she approached his side, he asked, "So, what did Vincent say?"

Jack had known when Vincent didn't readily leave that his friend/agent had a plan. It'd taken only one look at him talking to Elise to see what that had to be.

Vincent wanted to use Elise to get Jack to change his mind. He'd done that with Laney a few times too, but Jack was always onto him. So was Laney, for that matter. They'd often laugh and joke about Vincent's conniving, especially when he wanted to come along on a particular shoot. And they didn't blame him; he wanted a free vacation. Most folks did. Plus, they liked Vincent, so they typically let him have his way.

But this time, Jack wouldn't budge. And the quicker Vincent—and Elise—realized it, the better.

"Elise," he repeated brusquely, "what did he say?"

She filled him in on her conversation with Vincent, emphasizing what she learned about the ten percenters not getting paid if Jack didn't follow through.

Amazing, how much she'd learned in one short conversation. "Okay."

"Is that true, that they won't get paid?" Her brow knitted and that beautiful mouth turned down at the corners.

Jack wished he'd never kissed her, because it only reminded him of what he'd never do again.

"Jack, is it?" she repeated.

"Yes. It's true."

"How can you do that to those people? If you don't follow through with your end of the deal, they don't get paid. And really, that's not even the big picture, is it? This isn't about the money. It's about you, turning your back on your talent."

"I filmed the kids for you," he reminded her, trying to keep the bite out of his voice. "So I haven't turned my back on it completely, now have I? They'll have a Christmas appeal video that will be guaranteed to show people everything these kids have to offer and why they'd be crazy not to adopt them." In fact, although he'd never admit it, Jack had been moved to tears filming those precious kids. "They simply need someone to love them."

They'd been standing a few feet from the porch, and Elise moved to sit on the middle step, and then she put her elbows on her knees, clasped her fingers and bowed her head.

Jack didn't know if she were praying, crying or both. He took a deep breath, let it out and then sat beside her. She'd be leaving tomorrow. He'd made it this long without getting too close. He should tell her to go to Willow's Haven, then to Birmingham and then to have a nice life. Away from here.

Away from *him*.

In his head, he planned to say, "You should probably go," but then his traitorous mouth wouldn't cooperate.

"Elise, what's wrong?"

She looked up, and her eyes were swimming with unshed tears. "You, Jack. Vincent wants you to promote the movie. I do too. But it really isn't about the money. It's about your faith, and the fact that you didn't trust in it to guide you through the tough times."

"I lost my family. While they were on the way to a film that I clearly made for God. I'd call that more than tough times."

"That film, *The Journey*, do you know how many people you touched with that movie? And do you even remember the story? I mean, you directed it, right? Produced it? Whatever."

"I remember the story." How could he forget?

"Do you?" she questioned. "Because I do. And I'll tell you what I remember. I remember a movie where the opening scene had a man ready to end his life. He stood there, glaring at the light of an oncoming train. Then the light filled the screen, blinding the audience, until finally...we saw the moment his baby girl was born. We saw him hold her for the first time... at the moment his wife took her last breath."

Jack's throat clenched tight. He'd shot that scene countless times, until he'd clearly captured the pain in that new father's face.

"Then we watched that same man lose his

job, fight to keep his daughter when his in-laws wanted to take her away forever. And then he lost her. Lost custody. Lost a connection. And he'd turned to alcohol. And drugs. The man so alive and excited and overjoyed with the birth of his newborn daughter...lost it all."

She depicted the storyline with the same depth of feeling that Jack had intended upon filming.

"And then, after we followed him through one tragedy after another, you brought him back to that white light, to the oncoming train. Until, at the very last second—" she paused, looked at him with her eyes still glistening "—what happened, Jack?"

"His daughter saved him." Even as he said the words, he knew they didn't ring true. And so did she.

"Who saved him, Jack?" she asked. "Who really saved him? Because it wasn't her, was it? He thought about her then, visualized her growing up and getting married and having a baby of her own. And then he saw her searching to find him and the two of them reuniting. And he felt love. Forgiveness, when he forgave his wife's family. And peace."

She swallowed, touched his face. "Who saved him, Jack?"

"God did."

Her head moved in a slight nod. "You portrayed that so beautifully, how we can lose everything and still know that God cares, still let Him keep us safe from the storm."

She was right; he'd portrayed that on-screen. But directing a film about a man who lost it all was one thing. Losing everything he loved in the world was something else entirely. And Jack knew God had the power to do all things. He had the power to keep that plane in the air.

But He'd let it fall.

"Go to the screening, Jack. Go back to your talent." Her hand still rested against his face, and she slid it down to gently clasp his chin. "And back to God."

He couldn't give her what she wanted, couldn't give God what He wanted, either. "I...*can't*," he gritted out.

She stood, took a couple of steps and stopped. Jack watched, not wanting to look away in case this was the last time he'd ever see Elise Ramsey. She was angry with him, and that was probably a good thing. Then she'd leave. And he'd finally be alone.

She turned toward him, her face filled with disappointment, and some other undefinable emotion that made his heart stutter in his chest. "Let me tell you *why* I remember that film so clearly. Let me tell you about the two men who've most impacted my life."

Jack had no idea where this was heading, but he had a gut feeling he would not like it.

"Starting with my father."

Not what he was expecting. "Your father?"

She nodded. "Yes. My father had Asperger's. I grew up with a daddy that couldn't look at me when he talked to me. He didn't understand social cues, which would often embarrass my mother in public and cause the other kids at school to laugh when Dad attended any of our activities. It's tough, you know, to be the lead in the school's comedy and more people are laughing at your father in the audience than at you saying your lines."

He reached for her. "Elise, I'm sorry."

She took another step back. "No, I'm not finished. The year I turned thirteen, my mother decided it was too much, and she left him to marry a 'normal' guy. My stepfather was okay, but he wasn't my dad. And every time I would go see Dad, and see how alone he was, and how sad, I'd become more and more convinced that one day I would help people like him."

"Which is why you chose your profession, and work with children with forms of autism."

She nodded. "I want to help them learn to deal with it as best they can before they become adults. But helping my father wasn't enough." She visibly swallowed, and Jack could see that she struggled with whatever she was about to say.

"Elise, whatever it is, you don't have to tell me." She'd only talked about one man who had an impact on her life. That meant she had one more to go, and Jack didn't think he wanted to know about him. Whoever he was.

"Yes, I do." Her shoulders rose and fell with a deep inhalation, and then she eased it out and continued, "When I was twenty-five, I met Anthony. My husband."

Only one other time had Jack been so shocked by a single word, and that'd been when he'd received the news that his entire family was dead. "Your...husband." He'd assumed she wasn't married, but he should have known a woman like Elise wouldn't remain single. But she'd kissed him. She'd *kissed* him. And he'd come to know Elise well enough that he knew that wouldn't have happened if she were married. "But you aren't married now."

She shook her head, looked as though she wanted to say more, but her eyes had begun to fill with tears, and instead of speaking, she looked toward the sky and blinked several times to keep the emotion at bay.

A multitude of questions collided in Jack's mind, and he had a difficult time deciding what to ask first. But before he could utter a word, Elise gathered her composure and continued.

"He reminded me of my dad, had a hard time looking at me when he talked, a difficult time with social cues, and with life in general. But he was so kind, and he touched my heart. And…"

"And you wanted to help him get better." Jack didn't find it difficult to see how Elise would've been drawn to a guy like that after what she'd been through with her father.

"Yes," she admitted, "I wanted to help him get better."

Jack knew this conversation was too deep, too intimate and raw, exposing too much about this woman who would be out of his life soon. He hadn't wanted to lose anyone he cared about again, but the more he was around Elise, the more he cared.

Yet he couldn't stop her from speaking. He wanted to know everything about the woman he…

Jack wouldn't let himself complete the thought. Couldn't admit, even inwardly, that he'd let himself feel so much again. The more he felt, the more the sting when it all ended.

And it *would* end. Tomorrow.

"We didn't talk about having children the first few years we were married because Anthony said he wanted to make certain that he could handle the responsibility without it shutting him down. That's the way Anthony handled stress. He'd stop talking, stop working. He'd disconnect from the world, but every time that happened, I was able to bring him back around." She closed her eyes, then whispered, "Almost every time."

"What happened, Elise?" Jack asked the question, but he wasn't certain he wanted to hear the answer.

"He'd lost his job, not because of his disability but because they were downsizing. I had explained that to him, and he seemed okay about it. He'd even gotten a few hits for other positions. And he'd decided he was ready to try and have a baby. He said he'd never felt better." She sucked in a trembling breath, moved a hand to her mouth.

"Elise, maybe you shouldn't…"

"No. I want you to understand. I believed him, but he hadn't told the truth. He was worse than he'd ever been, and he blamed me."

"He blamed you? Why?"

"Anthony said I deserved a perfect family, one with a husband who could be counted on for stability, not only with his job but also with his mind, and he knew I wanted children, but he was afraid—" she took another ragged breath "—he was afraid they'd be like him. That's what he wrote on the note he left, that he had to end his life so he didn't do that to our kids."

Jack had sensed where the conversation was headed, but hearing her say it didn't lessen the impact. Her husband had killed himself… and blamed Elise. Jack felt for the guy, but he ached for Elise. And now he knew what had so desperately tormented her soul. "That's what you were crying about that day, wasn't it? When I first saw you in the woods?"

"I looked at the calendar that morning and realized—it'd been two years."

Jack stood, moved toward her and wrapped

his arms around her. "I'm sorry, Elise. I'm *so* sorry."

She sniffed against his chest. "You got me through that, Jack. *You* moved me past the pain and helped me to turn to God."

Jack had lost a key piece of the puzzle along the way. "Elise, what do you mean?"

"That movie, *The Journey*. I watched it that Christmas and saw Malachi go through all of those struggles, all of that pain, losing everything he cared about, everything he loved, and then God saved him. God let him see that his life wasn't over, that he had something to live for, to see his daughter again. And I realized that *I* could make it past my pain...with God's help."

She eased out of his embrace, enough that she could look at him directly. Her eyes weren't wet anymore, just filled with conviction. "Jack, you can do that for people, use the talent that God has given you to remind them that He is there, that He's always there, and He never leaves."

Mr. Simon—Jack—I have some terrible news. It's about your family...

Jack had been holding a long box he'd received from Laney's favorite florist. A corsage of yellow roses, her favorite, for her to wear to the premiere and tiny bouquets for the twins, daisies, their favorite flower, with baby blue bows. And he had a boutonniere for JJ. He'd asked Jack for one before, saying if he were wearing a tuxedo like his father, he should probably wear one of those little flowers that goes with it too. Jack couldn't wait to give them the flowers.

He'd been so excited.

Plane went down. I'm so sorry.

He was at the premiere. Ready to glorify God with the film that had been sparked by an incident with his son. His…son.

"Jack," she whispered, leaning back so that he saw her tearstained cheeks, and the quiet desperation in her beautiful brown eyes. "You can't—" her head shook as she spoke, and new tears sprang free "—you *can't* turn your back on God."

"I didn't." He backed away from the woman who had touched his heart so deeply but who pained him now, by asking him to go back when he couldn't. "He turned his back on me."

Chapter Ten

Savvy neared Elise's porch, where Elise had been reading her Bible most of the afternoon. After what had happened with Jack two weeks ago, she found this spot and this book comforted her like nothing else. God also managed, through His word, to remind her that she shouldn't put her faith in man, but in Him.

She'd put her faith in Jack, another broken man, and he'd torn her apart.

When would she learn?

Savvy, smiling, stepped onto the porch. "Where's Cody?"

Elise sighed. "Where he always is after school, at Jack's place, working on the car."

"Mark took him?"

Elise nodded. "He always does." Or rather,

he had since that last time she'd spoken to Jack, the day before Cody's IEP. Elise had been thrilled that the school wanted to hire her to remain with Cody for the remainder of the semester, until Christmas, as a resource guide, to help him transition to the new school. He'd transitioned easily and probably didn't need her anymore, but she hadn't relayed that information to the powers that be.

She liked being with Cody, even if he ditched her every afternoon in lieu of his other favorite person. She'd explained to him how she wouldn't be going to Jack's anymore, and Jack must have explained the same thing, because Cody hadn't argued. Which was good, she supposed, though she missed him when he was gone. And she missed Jack, more than she'd ever admit.

Elise wondered whether Cody would want to spend tomorrow, Thanksgiving, with his mentor, or whether he'd stay here for the holiday and celebrate with Elise and his friends.

She suspected he'd head down the trail.

"You've got a package," Savvy said, still grinning. "It's addressed to you and Cody, but I'm sure you can go ahead and open it."

"Me and Cody?" Elise marked her place in

the Bible and placed it on the small table beside her rocker.

Savvy plopped down in the other rocker and handed Elise the large manila envelope. Then she clapped her hands together beneath her chin. "Come on, I want to see what you think."

"You know what this is?"

"Let's just say I have a good idea." She leaned forward in her rocker. "Go on, pull the tab and open it."

Elise spotted the return address. "Damascus Entertainment?" Jack's old studio. Why would she be getting mail from them? Not only her, but Cody too.

"Savvy, what's this about?"

"It's okay. I know about Jack. I know who he is, and I know that's where he worked."

She knew? "How? When?"

"Vincent Farraday. He called and told me what was going on. It's so sad, what happened to Jack. But Vincent thinks this premiere will help."

"Did he say Jack was going?" A glimmer of hope pulsed through Elise as she pulled the long tab down the edge.

"No, he said Jack wasn't going, but then said he hadn't given up on him, something like that." Savvy pointed to the envelope. "And he needed to talk to me about your surprise."

Just the mention of a surprise reminded her of the day Jack had the Mustang delivered, and that moment when Cody spoke to them for the first time.

She smiled. He'd hardly stopped talking since.

"Elise, you're driving me crazy. Open it already."

She withdrew the contents and gawked at the folded cardboard—no, surely not. "Are these plane tickets?"

Savvy clapped her hands again. "Of course they are, silly! I had to call the State to get it approved for Cody to go, but they've agreed, because, I mean, it's such an incredible opportunity."

"To go where?" Elise looked at the flight information and raised her eyebrows. "LA?" Then she spotted the date. "In two days?"

Savvy nodded. "And your flight leaves pretty early Friday morning, so y'all should pack tomorrow, either before or after our Thanksgiving lunch. It'll beat watching football for sure."

"Los Angeles," Elise whispered, still dumbfounded by the tickets in her hand.

"Brodie said he can drive you to the airport in Stockville. I think the boarding pass was more for the appeal of the package than an actual necessity. You're going on a *private* plane!"

"How do you know all of this? And we're going to LA because..." She thought she knew, but she still wanted to hear it.

"Open the other envelope." Savvy pointed to a smaller red one that Elise had overlooked.

Sure enough, two tickets to the red-carpet screening of *Finding Home* were inside.

Savvy clapped her hands again. "So you're all set."

Elise had called Vincent after her meeting with Jack and told him that he hadn't had a change of heart. She'd apologized for not being able to help. She *hadn't* explained to Jack's agent that she'd never been able to help any man in her life and that she shouldn't have gotten so close. Shouldn't have thought that if she cared enough, he would listen. "Why would Vincent send us?"

"Apparently you made a good impression. And don't knock it. You're going to LA for a screening of the movie the whole world wants to see. Cody has a suit. Do you have a dress?"

"Not the kind I'd wear to this. Vincent didn't say anything about Jack going to the screening?"

"No, and we haven't got time to discuss it now. You have to pack, and we have to go shopping. You can't hit a red-carpet screening without a killer dress."

Chapter Eleven

Snow. Merely two weeks ago, Jack had filmed the Willow's Haven kids outdoors. But today had a chill in the air and a dusting of pristine white snow. Granted, it wasn't anything like the thick, white blankets he'd see if he lived in the northern states, but this was North Alabama, and even a light dusting was a real treat, especially for the kids.

Cody would love it.

He wondered what all the boy had done yesterday to celebrate the holiday. Thanks to the leftover fried Cajun turkey in Jack's refrigerator, he had at least some semblance that yesterday had been Thanksgiving. The trucking company that hauled the car had sent it as a thank-you for his business. A turkey. Jack had heard of people sending honey-baked hams for gifts, but never a turkey. And a big bird too, enough for a full-blown Thanksgiving dinner with all the trimmings.

Except Jack had dined alone.

Cody had invited him to Willow's Haven for the special meal, and Jack had nearly accepted the invitation, especially when Cody reminded him that it would be his first Thanksgiving without his family. But in the end, Jack hadn't been willing to do that to Elise. He was certain she didn't want him invading her holiday. Cody had told him she was staying at Willow's Haven until after Christmas to help him transition at the school, but he'd also said that Elise said he could come with Mark to see Jack from now on and that she wanted to stay at her cabin.

Cody had then asked him why she didn't want to come.

And Jack hadn't been able to give the kid an answer.

Because he was stupid? Because he was scared? Because he wouldn't forgive God?

Or all of the above.

Jack knew, but the pain in his heart wouldn't allow him to get over the past and move on to the future. Was it really because he couldn't forgive God for what He'd done? Or was it more because he knew he couldn't face the possibility of losing someone he loved again?

Or, more likely, was it both?

He glanced at the sole envelope on his kitchen counter. Had Vincent honestly believed sending him a plane ticket and a VIP ticket to the screening would get him to go? As if Jack needed a ticket to his own screening. He shook his head but couldn't hold back a smile. He had to hand it to the guy; he didn't give up. Which was one of the things Jack had always liked about the man.

Truthfully, he missed being around Vincent. Missed all of his director's team, in fact. And today, because he wouldn't show, they'd probably lose out on a year's pay. Or more.

An urge picked at his brain, that impulse to ask for help from the only One who could grant peace.

But He had let Jack down. More than let down, He had destroyed Jack's heart.

Still, for some reason, Jack felt a desire to talk to Him like he hadn't experienced in two years. And Jack wanted to be there for Vincent and his team. But how could he? He'd also wanted to be with Cody and Elise during the holiday meant for thankfulness, because he was so very thankful for the time he'd had with them.

But he'd ruined that chance too.

His chest tightened, throat grew thick. What had he done?

He missed them—both of them. Cody *and* Elise. And he needed them.

More than he ever thought possible.

The phone rang for the first time in days. Still reeling from the realization of how badly he'd messed things up, Jack glanced at the display. Vincent hadn't called after mailing the ticket, but he was calling now.

Jack didn't bother with hello. "I didn't get on the plane."

"I heard from the pilot an hour ago. I knew you didn't." Vincent didn't sound surprised, or disappointed.

"Vincent, I need to call you back later. I've got somewhere I need to go." He needed to get to Willow's Haven.

"A shame, though," Vincent continued, as though Jack hadn't spoken, "I'd hoped to surprise you with the other passengers."

Jack squeezed the phone. "*What* other passengers?"

"At least now I know Cody can keep a secret. Then again, he wouldn't have learned about the trip until two days ago. I'm guessing you didn't see him on Thanksgiving? He told me he'd invited you to Willow's Haven. Didn't go?"

"No, I didn't. Vincent, what—did—you—do?"

"I know he'd have loved going on the plane with you. And seeing the film."

Adrenaline hit Jack's veins so fiercely, his skin burned. "Cody," he managed, "is on the plane?"

"And Elise. From what I hear, they were thrilled to be one of the few to see *Finding Home* first. Though I know they'd have rather seen it with you."

Jack snatched the envelope from the counter. "You put them on a plane, Vincent? *A plane?* After what happened last time?"

Silence echoed through the other end.

"Vincent!"

"Jack, man, I didn't even think about that. But I've checked in with the pilot. Everything is going fine with their flight. And I'm sorry. I did what I thought would work to get you out here. We need you, Jack. You know that. And you need them, Elise and Cody." He exhaled roughly. "I saw it all over your face when I was there. I hear it in your voice when you talk about them. God put those two in your life to give you another chance at a family, Jack, and you're ignoring it. Following your own direction. God is trying His best to give you a happy ending, and you aren't letting Him."

Jack picked up the envelope, slapped it against the counter. "I didn't get on the plane. There is no happy ending here."

"Yeah, I didn't figure you'd get on the first one. I know you well, remember? There's another plane waiting for you in Stockville. If you get there within an hour, you'll make the screening. I've got a car on this end too, waiting to take you to the theater. Same way I got a car for Elise and…"

Jack had planned to head to Willow's Haven to show them what they meant to him, tell them what a fool he'd been. But he'd show them—tell them—today. Even if it took going to the screening.

He grabbed his keys and headed out the door.

Chapter Twelve

Jack still couldn't believe he would be attending the screening of *Finding Home* with Elise and Cody. And wearing a tux.

Vincent had the thing ready and waiting for him in the plane. He had to hand it to his agent; he went all out. And he did know Jack.

The pilot had already confirmed that Elise and Cody had landed safely and were on their way to the screening. They'd arrive for the prefestivities, the red-carpet photos and impromptu interviews with television crews, but Jack would be there for the show.

He wondered how Cody would like it.

And Elise.

An excitement rushed through him that he hadn't experienced in a very long time, but he recognized it immediately.

Anticipation. The moment he'd waited for, when the public got to see a piece of his heart and had the opportunity to see God the way Jack saw Him.

Because somewhere in the course of this season of Thanksgiving, Jack realized what a complete fool he'd been. God didn't take his family. God had been there, all along, through the storm. He'd been waiting for Jack to reach for Him, call for Him, and yet Jack had chosen to forego everything he'd claimed to believe and everything he'd portrayed on-screen.

Not anymore.

God, thank You for keeping Elise and Cody safe during their flight. And help me show them how much they mean to me. And forgive me, Lord. Forgive me for not having faith that You hadn't abandoned me. Let me never forget that again. And, Lord, if it be Your will, let my team forgive me. And, God, please, let Elise forgive me too.

He stepped off the plane to see that Vincent hadn't sent someone to pick him up. Vincent stood next to the black limo that would undoubtedly take them to the screening.

"Happy day after Thanksgiving, friend." He waved off the chauffeur and opened the door. "You forgive me yet?"

"I forgave you on the flight over." But Jack still punched his arm before climbing in.

Vincent laughed. "Now, that's the Jack I remember." He nodded to the driver. "Come on, let's go. He has a movie to watch and two special people to see." He winked at Jack. "Isn't that right?"

"That's right." Jack leaned his head against the seat, the flurry of events in the day hitting him and causing him to close his eyes as they made their way through typical LA traffic. Soon, he'd be with Elise and Cody again. And he'd show them the movie he was so proud of. Because he was proud of *Finding Home*, and he expected the public would like it as much or more than the previous films, because he had no doubt God had been there, guiding every scene.

The car moved slowly, which wasn't uncommon, but then they came to a complete halt.

Jack allowed himself to doze while they sat, until he realized they'd been still for quite a while, and he opened one eye. "What's happening, Vincent?"

"I knew it would be busy with people trying to get to the red carpet, but I can't remember it ever stopping traffic completely for this long when a screening was set to start. Especially if they're waiting for the director. They have to know you're en route."

The chauffeur had picked up his phone and started talking to a fellow limo driver who provided an update on the traffic ahead.

"There's been an accident," he said. "They're trying to get the emergency vehicles through. That's the holdup."

Vincent nodded, but fear shot to Jack's heart.

"Not again, Lord. Please." He grabbed his cell and dialed Elise's number. He hadn't called her and told her he was coming. He'd wanted it to be a surprise. But what if something had happened?

He vaguely heard Vincent ask the chauffeur, "Can you ask about the people involved in the accident? Anything at all? It's important."

Jack smashed the phone against his ear, gripped it so tightly his fingers stung. "Come on, Elise, answer."

More mumblings from the driver into his phone and then, "Yes, sir, it's one of the other cars from our company. He hasn't heard yet about the condition of the driver or the two passengers, a woman and a boy, yet."

Jack opened his door and started out. The thing was locked from the front and wouldn't budge. "Unlock this," he commanded. "Now!" He heard the lock disengage and climbed out, then started running...and praying.

Please, Lord. I'm begging You. Let them be okay.

Elise couldn't discern what had happened. One minute, she and Cody were riding in the car talking about the way they'd left snow in Alabama to arrive in hot and sunny LA, and then—Elise wasn't sure what had happened after that. There was a loud thunder. No, louder than thunder. And then she'd screamed. And Cody had yelled her name.

He'd yelled her name.

"Co-dy." Her throat didn't want to work.

"Everything is going to be okay. We need you to stay calm until we get you checked out."

Elise didn't know the man's voice. And she no longer heard Cody call her name.

"Elise! Cody!"

"J-Jack?" Now she *knew* she was dreaming. Jack was at his cabin. In Alabama. And she was certain that she and Cody had landed in LA. She remembered that clearly. The pilot.

Cody in his suit. And the satin blue gown she and Savvy had found at a consignment shop on the square in Claremont. She remembered all of that, but Jack wasn't in any of the equation.

"Elise!"

No doubt, that was Jack. But how?

It took everything she had to ease one eye open.

And see him, running toward her and wearing a black tuxedo, looking so tall and strappingly handsome. If she were dreaming, she really liked this dream. She decided to close her eyes and let it continue on.

Then she felt his hand on her cheek. "Elise, honey, are you okay? Tell me you're okay."

That hand felt so real. She forced a squint again.

There he was.

She tried to smile, but it hurt. Even so, she whispered, "You have the most beautiful eyes."

His relieved smile warmed her heart. "Elise, where's Cody?"

Cody. She forced her eyes wide, struggled to push herself upright.

"Miss, please. Let us do our job. And don't

worry, your son is okay. He's visiting with one of the firemen there, see?"

Elise turned to view Cody, standing at the front of a fire truck and discussing the engine with one of the firemen.

"Thank God," Jack said beside her.

Elise prayed this wasn't a dream. "Really?" she whispered.

He looked back to her, leaned down and kissed her softly. "Really. I don't know why it took me so long to see the truth, Elise. You told me. Vincent told me. But I had to figure it out on my own. God didn't leave me. He'd never leave me. He was waiting for me to let Him guide me through the storm." He gently stroked her hair. "And He led me to you. And Cody."

Her eyes filled with tears. "You came to the screening."

"I did."

"Okay, we believe everything is fine, but we're going to take you to the hospital just to make sure." The EMT adjusted something on the gurney.

"What about the screening?" she asked Jack.

"I'll let everyone know what happened and that I won't make the screening."

When she opened her mouth to protest, he added, "They will understand this, sweetheart, especially when I promise to make every other event on the press junket, including the Christmas premiere, which I plan to see with the woman I love by my side."

"The woman you love," she repeated, dazed.

"If she'll have me. But not only for the premiere, Elise. I don't want to be away from you for another minute. God has shown me how precious life is, and He's shown me how much you mean to me. I love you. I fought it, and that was crazy, because there's no denying how I feel about you. I love you, and I want to spend the rest of my life with you."

Elise started to answer, to tell him she loved him too, but her mouth stung, and she tasted a little blood. Then she put her hand to her face and felt dampness on her cheek.

"It isn't bad," he soothed, bending down and pressing a gentle kiss to her forehead.

"Your husband is right. Not bad at all. A couple of stitches, and you'll probably have a tiny scar reminder of the event, but I suspect you'll be just fine."

"A tiny scar to remind me of this day," Elise repeated. "Thank you, God. Because I never want to forget. And he isn't my husband," she corrected, "but he will be."

Jack nodded toward Cody, now dragging the fireman toward the gurney that held Elise. "You do realize this is a package deal, though, right?"

Her heart swelled as Cody neared. She'd been miserable at the thought of leaving him after Christmas, because she'd grown so very close to him and truly thought of him like a son. Now he would be a part of her life forever, as would this wonderful man whom she truly, deeply loved. "Oh, Jack, really?"

"Really."

"So this is Miss Elise and Mr. Amazing Jack," Cody said. "She was in the car with me when we were hit, but she's okay. The EMT lady said so. She said she just needed to rest a minute. Isn't that right, Miss Elise?"

It hurt, but Elise smiled. "That's right, Cody."

"We were in that car. It's a Maybach S600. It's made by Mercedes. It's a pretty cool car, and most people might think it's the coolest car they have ever seen, but they haven't seen our 1964 ½ Mustang. It's the most rare Mustang ever. But we have one. Do you want to know what all we did to the one Mr. Amazing Jack bought? We started with…"

"That's our boy," Jack said.

"That's our boy," she whispered.

"How soon do you think we can adopt him?" His hand found hers, and she squeezed it tightly.

"I hope very soon. Oh, Jack, this is so perfect. I can't imagine how life could get any better."

He lifted her hand to his lips, brushed a soft kiss across her knuckles. "Oh, I have one little idea."

"What kind of idea?"

The EMTs had moved on each side of her gurney and wanted to lift it up, but they too awaited Jack's answer.

"Do you trust me?" he asked.

She blinked. Not what she was expecting. Did she trust him? Trust him not to hurt her? Trust him to count on God whenever life dealt him a difficult hand? Trust him to come to her if he needed help and not attempt to handle things on his own?

She'd promised herself she wouldn't try to fix another broken man.

But then again, weren't we all broken without God?

And Jack had found his way through the storm, turned to God and found hope with Him, and with Elise and Cody.

She moved closer, brushed her lips against his and told him the truth. "Yes, Jack. I trust you."

Epilogue

Two years later

"Mr. Simon," a reporter yelled, as cameras flashed toward the red carpet, "can we expect another short film at the beginning of this movie about the Alabama children's home?"

"Yes, Mr. Simon," another called, "are you going to melt my heart and make me grab my checkbook again?"

"That's the goal." Jack smiled. "And Willow's Haven can always use your donations to help the children there, but the main goal of our short films for the home is to open eyes to the astounding possibilities of adopting or fostering God's children. You'll never know how much you can gain by loving a child until you experience it. And while you're giving them a chance at family, they're giving you so much more. The chance to love as God loves us. What's more beautiful than that?"

"See now, you're already making me cry." The journalist wiped her tears.

"Mr. Simon, tell us about *your* family."

Jack wrapped an arm around his wife, who turned and kissed his cheek. She was that way, always reminding him he was loved, and that he was God's first and hers second. He loved her even more for that.

"I'm happy to," Jack said. "This is my beautiful wife, Elise, our son, Cody."

"Cody Simon!" Cody yelled loudly. "I'm Cody Simon."

A few chuckles echoed through the crowd, but not because they were making fun of Jack's son; they, like Jack, adored the way Cody was so very proud of his new name.

"And that's my dad, Mr. Amazing Jack, but you can call him Jack Simon. I just call him Dad."

The little girl beside him giggled. "I call him Dad too."

"And what is your name?" the reporter, smiling, called.

"Naomi," she said proudly.

"Naomi Simon," Cody said. "She's my sister. But she isn't my *only* sister!" His grin stretched into his cheeks.

"What's that?" several reporters called out. "What did you say, son?"

They were all used to asking Jack about his family. Everyone loved the responses from Cody and Naomi. But this was a new bit, and they didn't miss a beat.

Jack and Elise had thought they'd wait until after Christmas to share their news that she was expecting, but it was the premiere of Jack's latest film, so why not? "Okay with you?" he whispered to his wife.

"Very okay," she whispered back.

"All right, then. Go ahead, Cody. Tell them our news."

"We're going to have a sister. She's supposed to come April 6, but they don't really know. She could come in March, or she could come later in April. And some people think she's most likely to come on a full moon, but we're not certain about that. But if she does come on a full moon, then the date would be either March 31 or April 29."

"Let's hope for March, then, Cody," Elise said, and Jack laughed.

He drew her close and put a hand protectively over her belly, joy and contentment flooding through him at the new beauty in his world.

"So, do you have a name for the new addition yet?" another lady called out.

"Naomi," Elise said, "do you want to tell them, since you picked her name?"

Naomi nodded, pigtails bobbing. "Her name…is Faith."

* * * * *

Pick up the first story in Renee Andrews's
WILLOW'S HAVEN *series:*
FAMILY WANTED

And enjoy these other sweet romances from Renee Andrews set in Claremont, Alabama:

BRIDE WANTED
YULETIDE TWINS
MOMMY WANTED
SMALL-TOWN BILLIONAIRE
DADDY WANTED

Available now from Love Inspired!

Find more great reads at
www.LoveInspired.com

Dear Reader,

While writing this book, I received a phone call I never wanted to receive. "I'm at the hospital." Those were Matt's words, and I could tell from his tone that it wasn't good news. If you've read anything about me or follow me on social media, you know that five years ago I met a twenty-four-year-old young man who needed a kidney and hadn't found a match. God put it on my heart that day that I would match, even though his family members hadn't. And God doesn't lie. We were a perfect, better-than-sibling, all-six-antigen match. Merely six months after meeting Matt, I gave him my kidney, and it began working in the operating room. Praise God!

Matt has become a son to me and my husband, a brother to our other two sons. We love him, his beautiful wife, Brittany, and their boys, our grandsons, Ryan and Brooks. They are family. So when Matt called to explain that he'd had a sinus infection and that the antibodies to fight the infection had viewed my kidney as foreign...and started attacking, my heart plummeted. My prayers skyrocketed. But as of today, the kidney has not started working again, and Matt has returned to dialysis.

One of the most painful things I've ever had to hear came a month ago, when Matt said, "I'm sorry. I hope you don't regret what you did, because you gave me a better life for five years and gave us two beautiful boys." I couldn't get the words out fast enough. "There are no regrets. Only blessings. Am I confused about why this is happening? Absolutely. We were the 'miracle match' as they termed us in the hospital and on the news. But God gave you five years with a working kidney. God gave me a son, a daughter-in-law and two more precious grandbabies. And God has been here, the whole time, working through the joy and the pain."

Will we face storms in life, the way Jack and Elise face storms in this book? Absolutely. But God never promised a perfect life, not here, though we will have that perfect life one day. Where we don't receive those hospital calls, don't watch our loved ones suffer, don't wonder what we could have done to have made things better. And until then, God is right here, all the time.

I wanted desperately to portray how much we need God in the stormy times of life. This book, these characters, have touched me so deeply, and I truly hope they've touched you too. And if you're facing storms, I pray for you to turn to God. Let Him be your anchor in the storm.

As always, I welcome prayer requests from my readers. Write to me at: Renee Andrews, PO Box 8, Gadsden, AL 35902 or through email at renee@reneeandrews.com and I will gladly lift your requests to our Heavenly Father in prayer.

If you would like to keep up with me, my family, my books and my devotions online, please join my Facebook page: www.Facebook.com/AuthorReneeAndrews

Blessings in Christ,
Renee

REQUEST YOUR FREE BOOKS!
2 FREE RIVETING INSPIRATIONAL NOVELS
PLUS 2 FREE MYSTERY GIFTS

Love Inspired®
SUSPENSE
RIVETING INSPIRATIONAL ROMANCE

YES! Please send me 2 FREE Love Inspired® Suspense novels and my 2 FREE mystery gifts (gifts are worth about $10). After receiving them, if I don't wish to receive any more books, I can return the shipping statement marked "cancel." If I don't cancel, I will receive 4 brand-new novels every month and be billed just $4.99 per book in the U.S. or $5.49 per book in Canada. That's a savings of at least 17% off the cover price. It's quite a bargain! Shipping and handling is just 50¢ per book in the U.S. and 75¢ per book in Canada.* I understand that accepting the 2 free books and gifts places me under no obligation to buy anything. I can always return a shipment and cancel at any time. Even if I never buy another book, the two free books and gifts are mine to keep forever.

123/323 IDN GH5Z

Name _____ (PLEASE PRINT)

Address _____ Apt. #

City _____ State/Prov. _____ Zip/Postal Code

Signature (if under 18, a parent or guardian must sign)

Mail to the **Reader Service:**
IN U.S.A.: P.O. Box 1867, Buffalo, NY 14240-1867
IN CANADA: P.O. Box 609, Fort Erie, Ontario L2A 5X3

**Are you a current subscriber to Love Inspired® Suspense books
and want to receive the larger-print edition?
Call 1-800-873-8635 or visit www.ReaderService.com.**

* Terms and prices subject to change without notice. Prices do not include applicable taxes. Sales tax applicable in N.Y. Canadian residents will be charged applicable taxes. Offer not valid in Quebec. This offer is limited to one order per household. Not valid for current subscribers to Love Inspired Suspense books. All orders subject to credit approval. Credit or debit balances in a customer's account(s) may be offset by any other outstanding balance owed by or to the customer. Please allow 4 to 6 weeks for delivery. Offer available while quantities last.

Your Privacy—The Reader Service is committed to protecting your privacy. Our Privacy Policy is available online at www.ReaderService.com or upon request from the Reader Service.
We make a portion of our mailing list available to reputable third parties that offer products we believe may interest you. If you prefer that we not exchange your name with third parties, or if you wish to clarify or modify your communication preferences, please visit us at www.ReaderService.com/consumerschoice or write to us at Reader Service Preference Service, P.O. Box 9062, Buffalo, NY 14240-9062. Include your complete name and address.

LIS15

REQUEST YOUR FREE BOOKS!
2 FREE WHOLESOME ROMANCE NOVELS IN LARGER PRINT
PLUS 2
FREE
MYSTERY GIFTS

☽☾☽☾☽☾☽☾☽☾☽☾☽☾☽☾☽☾☽☾☽☾☽☾

HEARTWARMING™

☆☆☆☆☆☆☆☆☆☆☆☆☆☆☆☆☆☆☆☆☆☆☆☆

Wholesome, tender romances

YES! Please send me 2 FREE Harlequin® Heartwarming Larger-Print novels and my 2 FREE mystery gifts (gifts worth about $10). After receiving them, if I don't wish to receive any more books, I can return the shipping statement marked "cancel." If I don't cancel, I will receive 4 brand-new larger-print novels every month and be billed just $5.24 per book in the U.S. or $5.99 per book in Canada. That's a savings of at least 19% off the cover price. It's quite a bargain! Shipping and handling is just 50¢ per book in the U.S. and 75¢ per book in Canada.* I understand that accepting the 2 free books and gifts places me under no obligation to buy anything. I can always return a shipment and cancel at any time. Even if I never buy another book, the two free books and gifts are mine to keep forever.

161/361 IDN GHX2

Name	(PLEASE PRINT)	
Address		Apt. #
City	State/Prov.	Zip/Postal Code

Signature (if under 18, a parent or guardian must sign)

Mail to the **Reader Service:**
IN U.S.A.: P.O. Box 1867, Buffalo, NY 14240-1867
IN CANADA: P.O. Box 609, Fort Erie, Ontario L2A 5X3

* Terms and prices subject to change without notice. Prices do not include applicable taxes. Sales tax applicable in N.Y. Canadian residents will be charged applicable taxes. Offer not valid in Quebec. This offer is limited to one order per household. Not valid for current subscribers to Harlequin Heartwarming larger-print books. All orders subject to credit approval. Credit or debit balances in a customer's account(s) may be offset by any other outstanding balance owed by or to the customer. Please allow 4 to 6 weeks for delivery. Offer available while quantities last.

Your Privacy—The Reader Service is committed to protecting your privacy. Our Privacy Policy is available online at www.ReaderService.com or upon request from the Reader Service.

We make a portion of our mailing list available to reputable third parties that offer products we believe may interest you. If you prefer that we not exchange your name with third parties, or if you wish to clarify or modify your communication preferences, please visit us at www.ReaderService.com/consumerchoice or write to us at Reader Service Preference Service, P.O. Box 9062, Buffalo, NY 14240-9062. Include your complete name and address.

WESTERN WP PROMISES

YES! Please send me **The Western Promises Collection** in Larger Print. This collection begins with 3 FREE books and 2 FREE gifts (gifts valued at approx. $14.00 retail) in the first shipment, along with the other first 4 books from the collection! If I do not cancel, I will receive 8 monthly shipments until I have the entire 51-book Western Promises collection. I will receive 2 or 3 FREE books in each shipment and I will pay just $4.99 US/ $5.89 CDN for each of the other four books in each shipment, plus $2.99 for shipping and handling per shipment. *If I decide to keep the entire collection, I'll have paid for only 32 books, because 19 books are FREE! I understand that accepting the 3 free books and gifts places me under no obligation to buy anything. I can always return a shipment and cancel at any time. My free books and gifts are mine to keep no matter what I decide.

272 HCN 3070 472 HCN 3070

Name	(PLEASE PRINT)

Address	Apt. #

City	State/Prov.	Zip/Postal Code

Signature (if under 18, a parent or guardian must sign)

Mail to the **Reader Service:**

IN U.S.A.: P.O. Box 1867, Buffalo, NY 14240-1867
IN CANADA: P.O. Box 609, Fort Erie, Ontario L2A 5X3

* Terms and prices subject to change without notice. Prices do not include applicable taxes. Sales tax applicable in N.Y. Canadian residents will be charged applicable taxes. This offer is limited to one order per household. All orders subject to approval. Credit or debit balances in a customer's account(s) may be offset by any other outstanding balance owed by or to the customer. Please allow 4 to 6 weeks for delivery. Offer available while quantities last. Offer not available to Quebec residents.

WPBPA16R